Unforeseen Predator

Who Wudda Thunk!

By

Donna Lea Anderson

This book is a work of fiction, inspired in part by real events. The characters, places, incidents, and dialogue are the product of the author's imagination and are not to be construed as real. Any resemblance to actual events, locales, or persons, either living or dead, is purely coincidental.

For more information contact
William Mays
Mays Publishing.
Books@mayspublishing.com

Original Cover by Donna Lea Anderson

Printed in the United States of America

ISBN 978-1733469616

Fiction: General

About Donna Lea Anderson

Born and raised in Corpus Christi, Donna Lea Anderson grew up admiring her hometown and all its amazing beauty. She loved the peaceful sunrises and bright orange sunsets, and the relaxing drives down Shoreline Boulevard. Few sights were as striking as the view from the Harbor Bridge, particularly at night. She enjoyed playful moments on the beach with sand between her toes and searched for unique seashells and sand dollars after a storm. Most of all she loved saltwater fishing with her rod tip bent reeling in a flounder, redfish, trout, and believe it or not black tip sharks.

When she ventured out of Corpus Christi, with her husband, Randy, God began to inspire her in so many ways she never thought possible. With pen in hand, she began to write and became a gospel lyricist, songwriter, and recording artist touching many with God's word.

Indeed, unknown talents, who knew!

God allowed her to enter the world through her mother's womb like many before and after. She believes we all are overseers of our souls, futures, ideas, beliefs, and accomplishments, not the world. So, with that said and in writing this book, and although fiction with several truthful events, her focus was to bring awareness about Sexual Abuse and how God plays a hand in giving us the ability to fend for ourselves or find a way to escape, emerging from the darkness of an Evil Predator.

Sexual Abuse has existed since the days of early biblical times and will continue for as long as the sun rises and sets in the world. As for Donna, a child victim at the hand of a Sexual Predator, she prays that God will forgive if one asks, and she believes that God always looks out for victims of Sexual Abuse whether they are little girls, women, little boys, or even men.

As a Christian, and as difficult as it may be, she reminds herself that God loves a forgiving soul!

Dedication

Inspire Yourself!

This book is dedicated to those, like me, who dream of becoming a Published Author, Songwriter, Recording Artist, or Freelance Photographer. I encourage all with ideas and the desire to tell a story to take time to listen and absorb your surroundings, whether day or night, truth or fiction, all it takes is one word, phrase, or paragraph to accomplish the goal of telling a story.

Like so many of you, I have God-given talents. Yet, my desire of writing a Novel and becoming a Published Author took over twenty years, and not to complain but life's everyday activities always came first. Now, years later and after allowing my imagination to soar, and after bringing my notes and ideas together I finally accomplished what I set out to do.

So, to all of you I say, always jot down your thoughts because unknowingly and amongst the pile of messy notes you may have a song or book in the makings.

Inspire yourself and God Bless!

TABLE OF CONTENTS

Introduction

Ok folks, it's time to kick back and read about two Texas women. Both love the Lord, and both endure somewhat similar occurrences. From birth their journeys are totally different with one struggling with evil from as far back as she can remember, and with the other growing up in a protective, happy, and loving family. Indeed, two different upbringings when both discover that evil is much closer than either one ever anticipated. The story involves romance, love, fear, hate, jealousy, deceitfulness, violence, and commitment all wrapped up into one story. As the Author, I will leave you with an important warning to consider and think about, and that is to know your own surroundings and know how to keep yourself safe. Now, enjoy the read!

Author: Donna Lea Anderson

Chapter One

I'm Done, Over, I'm Out of here!

On the eve of January 6, 1972, a full moon reveals tall palms swaying and whipping in the cold wind as a partially packed Greyhound Bus rolls into the Corpus Christi bus terminal, located downtown at Starr and Chaparral Street. After a long trip from a small town in West Texas the bus driver maneuvers his way through the terminal and searches for a convenient parking spot, and while doing so he announces there will be a twenty minute layover before leaving for Brownsville, Texas, the final destination of the evening.

Some folks are startled and some are awakened by the screeching loud noise that comes from the overhead intercom, and after a long ride from Little Wicked, Texas it seems a now stiff and cranky bus driver has the microphone way too close to his mouth. Again, he repeats his stern warning before opening the door. So, with the intercom cutting in and out his deep smoky voice indicates that he is a man of his word and means what he says.

Bus Driver Says,

Heed the warning folks I'm on a tight schedule, and I'll be leaving with or without you, "Twenty Minutes!"

Moans erupt throughout the cabin as a few unhappy passengers complain amongst themselves about the short layover. When the roar of the engine goes silent a handful of folks going on to Brownsville jump to their feet, exit the bus as fast as they can. Some run for the restrooms, and some grab a quick snack. Also wasting no time, is that somewhat cranky little bus driver as he flees from the bus and takes his place near the front exit, thanking all patriots for traveling Greyhound Trailways. Sure, that's part of his job but he also has a nasty little habit. Once out in the open air he pulls from his shirt pocket a long-awaited cigarette and quickly lights it up, savoring, inhaling, and exhaling every little puff of nicotine. Well, it seems the cranky little bus driver just isn't in need of a smoke, but he also likes to stretch his bones when he makes his scheduled stops.

As the cigarette dangles from his lips and in between puffs he bends over touches his toes, then makes several twist and turns, and once he believes that everyone is off the bus that's getting off he attempts to return to his seat. Well, not so fast. He doesn't get far and before he can make his way back to his seat, Lord and behold, there standing on the steps right in front of his eyes are two of the most beautiful legs he has ever seen.

Those beautiful legs belong to a woman named Charmaine Rene Davis, in her early thirties, an introvert, somewhat shy, homely and not much of a looker from the shoulders up. But the towering five-foot-eight blonde does have one thing going for her... a body that most women wished they had and a body that some men lust for in a woman. As Charmaine attempts to make her way down the steps the now creepy little bus driver can't seem to pass up an opportunity to put the moves on this homely looking wildflower with the most beautiful legs he's ever seen. So, he doesn't hesitate, quickly he initiates his moves and gives it his best.

Bus Driver Says,
Why hello there Darlin'.

Yes indeed, he has obviously done this before, and what a performance he gives as he flirts, winks, grinning from ear to ear as he lusts like a mad dog ready to take a poke at the first female dog available. He reaches out, offers a hand to help "Madam Legs" from the bus. With handbag and overly stuffed tote in hand Charmaine clutches them close to her bosom and steps from the bus ignoring his help and his "Yucky" advances. She also avoids any eye contact with this now proven to be jerk.

Charmaine Thinks,
You touch me creep and you'll be wearing my tote bag over your head.

He must tell by her expression how she feels because, shocked, he steps back and takes with him a little cloud of smoke lingering from what is now a nub butt cigarette, and after being shunned, he is not a happy camper.

Bus Driver Says,
Your loss Bitch!

Charmaine Chuckles to herself**,**
Maybe so, but when it comes to you buddy, I couldn't be so lucky!

Unsure where to go from here Charmaine is given directions to a cheap motel on Shoreline Drive. Not to waste money on a cab she sets out afoot in the cold and dark, walking to the motel recommended. The next day when dawn appears across the bay she awakes early, well rested, excited, and ready to start a new independent life for herself in Corpus Christi.

Reflecting back to Charmaine's past you could place Charmaine in the category of an adult runaway, raised by two not so loving parents and you may be wondering what she is running from. Unfortunately, it's physical, mental, and sexual abuse and the worst being labeled the towns prostitute from as far back as she can remember.

Yes, at a young age her parents turned her into a sex slave and during her developing years the two idiots found a way to make a few extra bucks while living off the taxpayers. With alcohol and drugs always ruling their state of mind they began pimping out their daughter and for years this became an easy way to pay for their own addictions. Sadly, this small-town girl now woman has been held hostage and brainwashed for her entire life and many would label these two parents not only as idiots but, "Filthy White Trash."

Often isolated from the world, Charmaine always felt there was more to life and, lucky for her, a little black children's Bible gives her hope. She keeps it hidden under her pillow and reads it as often as she can. Praying often, she truly believes that one day God's message of love will free her from the devil's bondage. Well, "Lo and Behold" one winter day in early January, He does just that, He answers her prayers.

One afternoon a blizzard roars through town as most of the

state. Charmaine is home alone when there's a knock at the door. With her parent's shady lifestyle, she's a little hesitant to open the door since her scheduled visitors never come by until after work and into the evening hours. After several knocks a little voice in her ear tells her, answer the door Charmaine. It's downright cold outside so she grabs a throw from a nearby chair and wraps it over her head and shoulders. When she opens the door, there stand two highway patrolmen looking through the screen door at her. Not sure why they are there, she's now scared as the house is cluttered with trash and drug paraphernalia. Quickly, she steps out onto the porch and pulls the door shut behind her. She sure doesn't want the officers catching a glimpse of what lies inside, because if they do she could find herself cuffed and being hauled off to jail. Doing her best not to appear nervous by their presence she begins to ask why they are there.

Charmaine Asks,
What can I do for you officers?

Officer Replies,
Sorry to bother you Ma'am but we have a few questions?

Charmaine, now leery, **Says**,
Ok, what can I do for you!

Officer Asks,
What is your full name, and do you reside at this residence?

Charmaine Replies,
My name is Charmaine Rene Davis and yes, I live here with my parents but, they're not at home right now.

Officer Says,
We know Ma'am that's why we are here. Regretfully, we are here to inform you that both of your parents were killed earlier this morning in a horrific car wreck off the main highway going into town.

For a moment time seemed to stand still, as the unexpected

news has left her speechless, she's in shock and doesn't even know how to respond.

Officer Says,
Ma'am, Ma'am… Are you ok? Do we need to call someone to come and be with you?

Charmaine hesitates a moment, then fakes a few tears **Responds,**
Uh… No Sir, I'll be fine I just can't believe they're dead, sniffle, sniffle, if you don't mind I'm going to go back into the house as it seems I have many things to take care of at this time.

By now the officers shiver uncontrollably and they are anxious to get out of the cold, but they are not sure if they should leave her alone since her response to the horrible news is just a little weird. Well, as weird as her response maybe, she is an adult and has just heard some of the most devastating news ever, which allows her to mourn in her own time and in her own way. Before they leave one officer hands her a sheet of paper which contains all of the morgue information. This will allow her to call and set up a time to go and identify the bodies at her own convenience.

Once inside and while she stands in the entryway, she wads up the paper and then tosses it across the room. With no more fake tears needed, she looks around the living room at all of the trash, clutter, and drug paraphernalia accumulated by her evil parents and their friends.

Charmaine Says to herself,
Wow, is this true or, am I dreaming? Am I really free from the devil's hold and from the two most worthless individuals in the world? I can't believe it, one minute they're here and another they're gone, removed from my life forever. Thank you, Lord!

When she hears the officers' car drive away, she runs into her bedroom and grabs that little black Bible, drops to her knees and head bowed calls out to her Father in Heaven.

Charmaine Asks,
God you've freed me, now what? Help me Lord; help me,

tell me what to do next.

At that moment she feels as if a ton of bricks has been lifted from her shoulders. Never wishing that her parents would be killed, God has been listening and has given her a way out of that horrible lifestyle. With so much happening at once it dawns on her that there are two local slobs coming by in a few hours expecting to see her parents and to have their weekly scheduled fling with her. She happens to be their routine stop before going home to their so-called better halves, their wives.

Charmaine Realizes,

Wait a minute… I don't have to do this anymore. I refuse to be a sperm bank for anyone, ever again… "I'm done, Over, I'm Out of here!"

With the sun starting to set she knows that it is way too late to gather up all that she will need to get out of town, and unfortunately she'll need to spend one more night in the house of the devil. So, she runs through the house, locks all the doors and windows, turns off every light and hopes when those scheduled slobs show up they will think no one's at home and leave.

At this point she can only hope and pray that they will do just that. Once all is secure, she locks and barricades her bedroom door with a chair. She's fearful to lie in bed because if one happens to force their way into the house, she knows her bedroom will be the first place they will go to. So, with her little black Bible in hand she nestles down in the dark closet for the evening. Patiently, she waits for that first unwanted knock at the door. Well, like clockwork and always on time she hears a car drive up and soon there's a knock at the front door. When no one answers the knocking gets louder, then silence. She doesn't move, she just holds her breath and hopes that she'll hear the car leave, but no such luck as now the devil pounds on the back-porch door too. Still, she doesn't move.

Charmaine Prays,

"Good Lord please let him leave, please!"

Within minutes, prayers answered again, and as the car speeds away the tires grind and chew up the loose gravel on the road.

She gives out a sigh of relief, one slob gone and one more to go. As she waits for the next slob to arrive her eyes become heavy as she starts to drift off to sleep. Wake up Charmaine there is no time to sleep now, the second slob is running a little late and is now pulling up in front of the house. Well, as expected and like the first slob he too is not happy when he finds the house dark and no one home to answer the door. He also tries the back-porch door and soon he becomes one furious slob, as he rants, and raves, with one curse word after another because he can't get what he paid and came for. Once again, she doesn't move, praying he too will leave and lucky for her, he does. Unsure if one or both may return, she decides to stay put and spend the night in the closet hidden under some filthy dirty sheets and blankets. Indeed, the smell is ungodly gross but at the moment this is where she feels the safest.

After sleeping through the night she awakes screaming at the top of her lungs and it seems one cold little field mouse has found its way into her closet. Like her, he too is trying to stay warm when the unwanted varmint attempts to snuggle up with her. From under the covers she wrestles with the little varmint but he's not leaving as she kicks the door open then slings him and the covers across the room.

Charmaine Cries out saying,
Lord please, get me out of this filthy horrible place, please!

Then, as the unwanted varmint makes his getaway through a small crack in the floor the phone rings scaring the holy moly out of her. She is hesitant to answer but does. It's the landlord. He heard about her parents and plans to come by after lunch to discuss future rent payments and unfortunately, back payments owed. Once she gets him off the phone, she starts to throw things, stuffing as many clothes as she can into an oversized tote. Once her tote and handbag are stuffed with clothes, Bible, and a few small trinkets she puts on her raggedy polyester coat, wraps a red scarf around her neck, and heads for the front door. But, just short of leaving out the front door and before she can turn the doorknob she remembers the most important thing that she needs.

Charmaine Says,
Oh shoot, I need money and now, where did those two old

fools hide all of the dough?

Well, lucky for Charmaine and due to her parents' unlawful lifestyle, they never used the one and only bank in town, choosing to keep their business transitions private. Over the years and as far back as she can remember, any and all income was hidden throughout the house and never revealed to her as to where it was stashed. This was done since Charmaine's body brought in the big bucks and fearful that if she knew its location she may up and leave one day taking all of the money with her.

So, with the money issue keeping her from leaving and the clock ticking, she has to search for the hidden treasure and do it fast. She starts with the living room couch, flips the cushions off onto the floor and finds a mere five dollars and some small pocket change. She knows that won't get her far and now desperate she heads for the hoarders' cozy sanctuary, their bedroom. After totally destroying the living room, their bedroom, and one bath she runs to the kitchen. There she searches inside the refrigerator and opens all containers, shelves of pots and pans, dishes in cabinets, under the sink, and a half full trash can, but nothing.

Then, she puts two and two together when she recalls what her Dad always called his pimp money; "Sugar Money," and there on the kitchen cabinet in plain sight sits a large canister full of sugar. She shoves the flour, tea, and coffee canisters out of the way and bingo, inside is a wad of tens and twenty-dollar bills, four hundred and eighty dollars to be exact. Amongst the sugar it's tightly secured with a rubber band and wrapped in plastic wrap.

Disappointed by the find and expecting more, time is wasting and there is no time to search further. Sure, she could probably find more in the attic if she had time, but she's got to get going before the landlord arrives. Now with only four hundred and eighty-five dollars and some small pocket change in hand she bundles up and hits the road walking to the nearest bus depot.

Once there she hops onto a bus which will take her to Corpus Christi Texas in search of a new and better life. Since there's a five-hour trip ahead of her, and with Little Wicked, Texas drifting on the horizon she finally gets to relax and unwind for a bit. As the bus rolls down the highway she jots down on the back of her ticket stub, a few important goals. First, find a cheap place to live. Second, find a job. Third, get her G.E.D. since she dropped out of High School years ago and never finished. With a plan in place and not much scenery to look at she tilts the seat back closes her eyes and daydreams of her soon to be new life in Corpus Christi.

Chapter Two

New Beginnings in a New Town

Within days Charmaine rents a cheap garage apartment located near six points (six roads that inter meet at one intersection). It's not the Taj Mahal but compared to what she was raised in, it feels and looks like it. Lucky for Charmaine the above garage apartment is furnished with a small television and phone. It is also within walking distance to her new job waiting tables at Shepp's Diner, a twenty-four-hour diner located in the six point's area. The pay isn't great which means she will have to rely on tips to help pay the bills.

It doesn't take Charmaine long to fall in love with Corpus Christi and her new surroundings. Her weary, damaged soul finds comfort with the towns swaying palm trees, sea gulls, and thick, salty breezes blowing off the bay. Her walk to and from work isn't too bad but waiting tables and standing on her feet for eight hours or more isn't easy. As tough as life is, when it comes to Charmaine, she never complains even though her feet hurt and back aches continuously. She looks at it this way: no need to complain, a girl's got to do what she's got to do to make money, and in a lawful way. Even though money is tight, she strives forward, works hard, wasting none, and saves every little extra nickel and dime that comes her way.

Immediately, Charmaine becomes a model employee at work, and though the job has its disadvantages, it keeps her lawful and off the streets and from returning to prostitution. After being raised as a prostitute and held hostage for her entire life the opportunity and desire to let her light shine and be a good example for others is extremely important, she desires and is ready for the Christian lifestyle which she was always denied.

Although a model employee she now has a few personal issues to deal with. She quickly learns that life outside of Little

Wicked can also be just as tough, as her shyness and being an introvert stand in her way of mingling and befriending others. So, as the new employee and as she struggles with her inner demons, she finds that most at work are friendly, and even her Boss comes across as a perfect gentleman, treating women with respect. For Charmaine this will take some getting used to, since she's never been around men who act and show their gentlemen side.

In most working environments once the new employee is hired it seems there's always one or more co-workers who will emerge from the shadows and start to show their true side. Well, unfortunately for Charmaine there is a diner bully in her mist, ready and waiting to attack from the bunch. When it comes to bullies, they are usually jokesters, and label themselves flawless, and love to target teasing others. They seem to get great pleasure as they indulge in the moment as they find joy when making fun of one's looks, speech, and overall appearance.

Within days of her employment and sooner than expected, one morning Charmaine is caught off guard as she gets the privilege of meeting the diner's bully. The bully "Bootzy" (folks call her since she loves to wear boots) has been on vacation and has returned rested and ready to pounce on the new employee named Charmaine. It's clear that she has already been informed about the new waitress in town. Seems Bootzy with the baby doll face and attractive figure is already feeling threatened. Charmaine is within minutes of finding out that Bootzy is an absolute idiot and soon proves that she doesn't have too many smarts between the ears. After one look at Charmaine's bosom and long beautiful legs, Bootzy nudges Charmaine off into the break room in the back.

With no one around Bootzy immediately goes off into a jealous verbal attack. Charmaine is in awe, and not sure who this woman is. She just listens and lets her get whatever off her chest. Bootzy is totally overwhelmed with anger. The plan is to intimidate her victim, she attacks Charmaine's age, poking fun at her homely looks and proceeds to make it clear that she is the head waitress at the diner and not to overstep her bounds when certain customers come in. You see, Bootzy, a married woman in name only, likes to flirt and cutup with certain male customers and there is no way she's going to allow anyone to move in on her high-tipping customers. Before Charmaine can reply to the little twerp's nonsense the Boss peaks in through the door.

Boss Says,

Ok ladies, Bootzy, Charmaine, enough with the chit chat, times wasting get to work.

Thanks to the Boss, Charmaine now has the name of the little twerp, and when it comes to her personality, the woman is obviously delirious and has proven that she is nuts. Well, I guess that earlier encounter wouldn't fall under a formal introduction since throughout the day there's nonstop harassment with many insults and looks to kill.

As days go by, and when Charmaine is scheduled to work certain shifts with Bootzy, she struggles with staying calm and finds it extremely difficult to be around her. Unfortunately, the gal doesn't let up, and avoiding her is absolutely impossible, "PERIOD!"

Author:

You may be wondering why Bootzy doesn't get fired?

Well, Bootzy isn't as dumb as she acts, she knows when to attack and when not. She's like the lion who stalks its prey before attacking, and when the Boss isn't around and when opportunity allows, this lioness steps up her game. Verbally, she attacks her new victim in front of certain male customers who are those high-paying tippers. Obviously flirty, Bootzy just isn't a bully, but she is a greedy one at that, and wants all of the attention and tips to go to her and her alone.

Author:

Like me, you may be wondering what else she may be getting from them, besides tips.

With that said, one day at lunch and while the diner is full of hungry customers, Charmaine comes face to face with two of Bootzy's high-paying tippers. They sit in their usual spot, at the bar. The two hunkie-lookin' guys are young in their mid or late-twenties, masculine carpenters, tall and good-looking with one blonde and wearing a "Yanks" hat and the other with dark curly hair. Just two buddies looking for a few laughs while grabbing a bite to eat while trying to impress the ladies with their lingering stench of cheap cologne.

Charmaine does her best to ignore them, but they keep trying to hit on her. Noticing from across the room, Bootzy hurries over to interrupt the small talk between them all. Yikes, where is the Boss when you need him? Well, he's in a back room checking inventory which means he'll never see or hear a thing. So, with him out of the picture other waitresses split and high tale it for the break room as Bootzy dives right in. Her potty mouth spews out one hateful insult after another and it is obvious she is one furious woman. Charmaine's face turns bright red, embarrassed by what she is saying while Bootzy and her hunks crack up laughing. Charmaine chooses to play nice, walks away and totally ignores Bootzy and her smart mouth. Yep, she refuses, vows to never give her and her hunkies the time of day.

Author:

Well, lucky for Bootzy, "The Good Lord" has His hands on the shy introvert because if He didn't, I truly believe that with one good punch to the nose Charmaine could have knocked that little twerp sailing across the room, never blinking an eye.

On Thursday January 27th Charmaine is up early and once dressed she walks to work as usual. Wearing her raggedy polyester coat and red scarf, she makes her way to work as she munches on a dry piece of toast while enjoying the fresh crisp morning air. It's a little nippy outside, but nippy doesn't bother her, remember she's from West Texas where nippy feels pretty darn good to some folks. Today she is scheduled to work her favorite shift, nine to five which means she'll be home before or right at dark.

Once at work the day flies by. The diner is hopping, totally busy, and with her shift coming to an end she begins to dread the walk home. Earlier in the day a cold front blew in from the northwest with the temperature dipping way into the lower forties. From what some customers say the weather is going to get much colder with rain into the night.

So, after she hears that bit of news and in-between waiting on customers, she watches through the diner windows as the wind howls and blows and then makes its way down the street. At times the wind sneaks and creeps inside the diner when the door opens and closes. Soon, the wind begins to throw a fine mist of rain on everything that gets in its way and the sidewalks are becoming slick making it absolutely miserable for all that want, or have, to be out in it.

Unfortunately, and soon, poor Charmaine is going to be one of those folks. With her shift ending soon she randomly glances down at her trusty "Timex Watch" which she wears daily. She also watches the front diner door expecting to see her relief waitress walk through the door so she can get home before the weather gets worse.

Author:

Can you guess who the relief waitress is, and if you said Bootzy, you're right. Now here's something to think about, is this bully capable of calling in sick since she despises Charmaine so much? I would say, indeed she would, and I'm sure most would agree.

Well, if you said yes then you're sort of right, because soon the Boss receives a call and thankfully the news isn't all that bad. Bootzy is not sick but as usual she is running late.

Charmaine Mumbles under her breath,

"Darn that woman!" I bet she's running late on purpose.

Then comes the one thing she didn't want to hear under the circumstances. The Boss needs her to stay until "Queen Bootzy" arrives. Charmaine is not happy with that bit of information; she bites her tongue hoping he won't pick up on her anger. So, being the new employee on board and wanting to please the Boss, the only thing to do now is to pitch in and take care of the overwhelming flow of customers.

Author:

When the weather is bad, I'm always amazed and finding it odd... Why do folks love to venture out challenging "Mother Nature" at its worst, wanting to shop and eat out? What happened to staying at home and cozying up with a warm fluffy blanket, safe and watching a great movie or reading a good book?

Well Hallelujah! Better late than never and just an hour late, Bootzy finally shows up. She makes a mad dash through the diner apologizing over and over to the Boss. Not wasting any time, she straps her apron around her waist and gets right to work. Deliberately, she shuns Charmaine who stands in her wake and of course Charmaine does her best not to collide with the "Queen of Bullies."

Charmaine scurries to the break room, rips off her apron, and tosses it into a dirty clothes hamper. Then quickly, she slips her coat on over her slightly stained pink uniform and wraps her red scarf around her neck. She's so glad that she chose to wear all after being unaware of a strong cold front blowing in later with such a vengeance. Once she is buttoned up, "Snug as a Bug," she makes her way to the front door entrance of the diner. The Boss stands at the cash register and after change is given to a customer he goes out of his way to thank her for staying over and also offers her a ride home if she wants to hang around for another hour. Now too tired to wait and with it getting darker outside she just wants to get home, and graciously declines his offer.

As soon as she steps out the door, a blast of cold freezing wind almost knocks her off her feet. She wrestles with the door trying to make it secure before she walks away.

Charmaine's Thoughts:

"Helloow there... old man winter." Maybe I should reconsider the Bosses offer? Nah, come on girl, you can do this.

With the door secure she begins her journey home and it's time to kick-it-in-gear as she walks brisk fully with old man winter showing no mercy as he pounds her from all directions. At times he's a tough old guy as he whips her over and over trying to throw her off balance. Charmaine hopes to be home within twenty minutes or less and prays her calculations are right.

Charmaine Says,

Come on feet time to move, gotta get these tired old bones home.

With the change in the weather, she truly wishes that she had a car, but that's "NOT" happening anytime soon. Charmaine, just keep wishing and walk. As she continues, thank goodness for the streetlights which reveal all cracks and uneven concrete that lie in her way. Worried about stumbling, her main focus is on where and how each foot lands. Soon her neck scarf begins to loosen. With a blinding cold mist making it difficult to see she stops to tighten it up.

As she fumbles with her handbag and tugs to tighten her scarf, she realizes that she is standing in the middle of a long narrow road. But it's not just a road it's an alleyway made of loose gravel and one that she is not familiar with. Curious and wondering where it leads the mist has lifted a little and she can now see a towering dim light pole and a few cars that pass off in a distance. Shivering in her tracks she thinks this alleyway may be a shortcut straight to her apartment. But not sure where it really leads her gut tells her… "Stay on your familiar path Charmaine, stay on the familiar path." She does so, but not so fast, after a few more steps her curiosity gets the best of her.

Charmaine Says,

Oh, what the Heck! I'm freezing and I'm going to take a chance on this little alleyway.

Now, and after a spontaneous decision has been made, she gives one last tug on her scarf which is now snug and not going anywhere. As she makes her way down the alleyway, she quickly slides her long slender fingers back into her pockets trying to protect them from the frigid weather. So, combined with the weather, darkness, and unsure of where she will end up, she begins to feel a little leery about her decision.

At that moment she can only hope and pray that the odds are in her favor as she anxiously heads for home. With the alleyway being narrow there are homes and garages which bring some relief from most of the brutal wind, but overhead that's another story. The back yards are full of shrubs and tall leafless naked "Ash Trees" that whip franticly in the howling wind. Back and forth the limbs sway overhead while some cold wind creeps in-between the garages and adjoining homes.

With dim residential lights shining randomly in-between the garages there are shadows everywhere, which makes this journey a little spooky and downright scary. Amidst the "Spooky and Scary"

Charmaine keeps on walking and focuses on the other end of the alleyway. Soon, a few trash cans begin to roll freely around her, and it seems the wind or a stray animal is browsing through the trash cans searching for a bite to eat. The noisy ruckus causes a few neighborhood dogs to go on alert, barking, which causes her heart to pound uncontrollably. For someone who is scared to death of dogs, just the thought of white fangs trying to chow down on her is not so good. Talk about being in the wrong place at the wrong time, well, this is one of those times. Whether be wind or animal causing the ruckus, at this moment it doesn't matter, she is downright scared and is starting to regret her spontaneous decision.

Charmaine Says,

Ok girl, no time to stop and check the old heart rate, you gotta get out of here, move it and move it now!

Author:

Well, I'm sure you would agree, any trash can rolling in the wind at night and not secure is definitely at the wind's mercy and as for the dogs growling and barking? Absolutely, that's just what they do when a strange intruder passes through their own personal territory.

Continuing down the alleyway she does her best not to show fear when a few more vicious dogs begin to bark, growling as they try to lunge over the fence at her. Desperate to run, she doesn't. She just takes longer strides trying to escape. Once past their area and after several attempts to get at her, all unsuccessful, the dogs calm down. Indeed, her being in the alleyway has made many of these four-legged critters unhappy as they want her to be gone, and at this moment, she is more than happy to oblige.

Even though the dim light at the end of the alleyway is getting much closer, the dogs and scary noises have made her more than desperate to get out of the alleyway. Poor Charmaine, and I'm sure you would agree, it is quite obvious that she should have stayed on the familiar path which led home. Well, it's too late now to change her mind so she strives forward trying to reach the light pole but, not so fast Charmaine. It seems your spontaneous decision is about to get much, much worse.

From out of nowhere footsteps approach from behind. Terrified and before she can turn to see who it is, its lights out for Charmaine. Within seconds and with little warning she is on the ground knocked out cold, hit with an unknown object which knocked her totally unconscious. Shortly, she goes from unconsciousness to semi-conscious and as difficult as it is to comprehend, she realizes that she is no longer on her feet walking but lying flat on her back.

After being dragged out of the alley and into some nearby shrubs she finds herself dazed and unable to move or speak due to the agonizing blow to the back of the head. Her pain is excruciating, and her vision blurred. As she lays there, she knows someone is near because she can hear him, feel him, and— smell him. She begins to moan and hopes that someone has come to help her but, as you may have guessed help has not arrived and it doesn't take her long to figure out the inevitable, this person is there to rape her. It seems the West Texas lifestyle has followed her to Corpus Christi and as miserable as she feels, if possible, she is not going to let this rape happen. She began to fight back and tries to push the brute off but is unable.

Charmaine Screams Out!
"No! No! STOP!"

Quickly, a hand covers her mouth which prevents her from calling out. He is a strong individual and has her arms and torso pinned down to the ground leaving her helpless and unable to move. While tears begin to roll down her face, she can't believe that she has just fallen victim to another despicable individual.

The sexual abuse seems to last forever when suddenly it's over and all she can do now is remain still and pray that he just goes away, not killing her. Still atop her, the attacker's heavy body goes limp; he's out of breath and needs a moment to catch it. As they lay there, she can only wish that she had the strength to push him off, but she is just too weak from the entire trauma.

Finally, the gutless weasel gets to his feet and with her legs spread he now stands between them with his back turned to her. Charmaine chooses to remain still, silent and hopes he will be leaving soon. Cold and shivering, he reaches to pull up his pants which are cuddling around his calves.

Once he has his pants up, he seems to struggle with the zipper before buttoning up his coat. Then, it seems he has lost something as he quickly turns around desperate to find it. While he scans the area a dim light shines on them both and God only knows, where that dim light is coming from.

There it is, lying next to Charmaine and it's a royal blue hat with the logo "Yanks" on it. He slaps it to his leg removing the dust and then places it back onto his head, but before he can make a quick getaway, he realizes that she saw his face.

The "Yanks" hat is a dead giveaway and Charmaine can't believe who the guy is. No doubt in her mind, he is one of Bootzy's high-tipping customers, and he wears that "Yanks" hat, faithfully never taking it off. It seems the search for the hat turns out to be a good thing for Charmaine because she can now identify this jerk. She doesn't know his name, but it seems he has strayed from the infamous Bootzy's arms.

Author:

Well, all I'm goanna say is, "BUSTED!"

One may call it luck, but Charmaine truly believes that God intervened allowing just enough light to shine, so that she could identify him. But that may not have been such a good thing as this sexual assault is about to go from rape to one of those "Oh my goodness" moments.

As she remains silent lying on the ground and stunned by who the attacker is, the evil brute with his masculine body, good looks, and cheap cologne continues to stand over her piddling with his coat buttons. Well, so much for luck, because by the look on her face, it's obvious to him that she knows who he is and immediately the situation changes.

Forget about the buttons, he is not a happy camper and immediately goes into an angry rage. Quickly, he drops to his knees, straddling Charmaine's cold and tortured body, putting them both in an eye-to-eye situation. Charmaine remains still, fearful to move, and she even attempts to hold her breath since the stench of alcohol on his breath mixed with the cheap cologne is more than overwhelming. In a drunken, furious rage, he pulls in close to her face, violently grips and squeezes her jaw, he warns her, and he threatens her, making demands, while poking at her nose with his index finger.

Attacker Says,

Look you homey-looking slut, if you ever and I mean ever, tell anyone what I did. Oh no, let me make this clear, what we, you, and I did, I will come after you, hunt you down like a mad dog, slit your throat, and kill you with no hesitation. Also, I won't stop there; once you're dead I will cut you up into a thousand little pieces, and then stuff you into one of my extra-large trash bags from my truck.

Soon, and out of nowhere he cries out this creepy little laugh.

Attacker Says,

Don't assume that's all, because the best part will follow when I take you atop the Harbor Bridge and toss you over into the ship channel, and it will be all over, adios forever.

Wow, this guy has just proven that he is much crazier than his nutty waitress Bootzy. Once he's made his threats known, he reaches around and grabs a hand full of her hair pulling her face even closer to his. Lip to lip he gives her a wet slobbery kiss, and then with his tongue he licks her face as if she were some kind of favorite lollypop.

Attacker Says,

You best remember what I said, you old slut, tell no one. You got it?

When she doesn't respond he vigorously shakes her head and grits his teeth saying, you got it, slut?

Charmaine, voice quivering, still in tears **Says,**

I got it! I got it!

Attacker Says,

That's good... Say, maybe we can hook up again sometime, wha'da you think?

Then there's that creepy laugh again and before making a quick getaway he slams her head back to the ground hoping that he has knocked her out for a second time. Remarkably, NOT! She just lies there and listens to the fading sounds of his footsteps while he runs from the scene. For the second time that night the dogs growl and bark while an evil rapist escapes into the night.

Shortly, after he is gone and when the dogs calm down, oh so gently she attempts to sit herself up. She moans and groans and as expected it's not very easy.

She braces herself against a nearby garage and tries to pull herself together. She's wet from head to toe, dirty, her head hurts, and she literally feels as if a semi-truck has just plowed over her entire body. So, all alone in the dark she just sits there sobbing uncontrollably with her panties now ripped and barely hanging from around one ankle. With the cold misty rain starting to freeze she needs to get up and get home immediately. There are a few shrubs at arm's reach, so she uses them to pull herself up which brings her to her feet. Once standing she pulls her dress and coat down from around her waist and hopefully this will be the last time she has to adjust that red scarf. Very carefully she bends down to slip her ripped panties off from over her shoe and after a little twisting and turning she gets it done. She shoves them into her coat pocket and plans to throw them away later. Soon she makes her way toward the alley road and after she takes a few steps she realizes that she doesn't have her handbag. Panic engulfs her train of thought as it is extremely vital that she find it, as her apartment key is inside.

Charmaine Says,

Oh God! Where's my handbag? I need it Lord, Help me find it.

Unlike her attacker searching for his favorite "Yanks" hat, she definitely needs that key inside the handbag. Well, a blessing from God comes after she takes a few more steps, stumbles over the handbag and what a relief it is. It's now dirty and crushed after the attack but the clasp is still closed, a good sign that the key and a few other items are still safe inside. Too dark to check now, she'll deal with the key issue when she reaches her front door. Soon, she's back in the alleyway and proceeds gingerly, walking toward the dim light pole that she once focused on before the lights went out. Each step is painful, as she cries. Quietly she moans and groans not wanting to get the dogs all riled up again. At times she uses her coat sleeve as a hankie as she wipes the tears from her face and freezing snot from her nose. She prays and prays that the alleyway will give her a pathway home. Then, when she reaches the dimly lit light pole, she leans on it for a moment, also discovering that she was right, for her apartment is right across the street.

Author:
Her key you may ask.

Yes, it's in her handbag along with lipstick and five dollars and twenty-five cents which proves that her attacker wasn't out to rob her. Once inside of her apartment she quickly secures the deadbolt behind her. Her head pounds nonstop and she needs something for the pain, but before she takes any pain medication, she needs to secure her apartment, worried the rapist may have followed her home.

Not taking any chances she grabs a chair from the kitchenette table, tilts it, and shoves its backside up under the doorknob. Now, she feels safe, so safe that it would take more than muscles to get through the door. It's now late in the evening and after she takes something for the pain, she stands in the shower scrubbing her body from head to toe, desperate to remove the stench of the scum ball's cheap cologne.

Emotional, her tears turn into anger as she whips that shower curtain open and grabs her clothes from the floor… Yep, into the shower everything goes, scarf, dress, bra, and even the polyester coat with panties still in the pocket. In a rage of anger, she rips them out of the pocket. She begins to stretch them, wanting to rip up the remaining parts not damaged by the rapist, and once she's done, she tosses them into a little trash basket next to the tub. With the panties now filed in the trash basket she continues to scrub herself and her remaining clothes. Scrubbing the other clothes in a frenzy the new bar of soap quickly becomes a little puddle of bubbles. Once the clothes have been sterilized, she takes a moment to stand under the shower head, and with her hands now pressed to the wall the gentle trickles of warm water seem to bring a calmness to her regretful soul. She begins to question herself after making such a foolish spontaneous decision.

Charmaine Questions herself,

Why Charmaine why, why did you ignore this imbecile's stares and flirtatious remarks when in the diner and Bootzy wasn't around? How stupid you are. How could you allow yourself to fall victim to this disgrace of a man, you of all people should have known better.

It seems some victims have the tendency to blame themselves when something bad happens and Charmaine has become one of those people. She is furious and mostly at herself for not seeing the signs. For weeks now and right under her nose he sat in the diner, flirting with Bootzy, and at the same time eyeballing her and planning to rape her when opportunity allowed. Sadly, and unfortunate for Charmaine, he put his plan in motion tonight.

In the process of drying off she considers calling the police, but when she recalls what he said she decides not to since she's not even sure if the Corpus Christi authorities would believe her when they learn about her horrible past. They could be just as corrupt as Little Wicked's authorities. Not wanting to go there she decides to leave well enough alone and move on with her life.

Author:

Wow, plans to leave well enough alone? Not so sure about that, I guarantee if that scum ball ever tries it again, she'll kill him.

After she hangs up her dress, scarf, and coat so they can dry overnight, she pops a few more extra strength pain meds before jumping into bed. Worn-out physically and mentally she lies in bed desperate to fall asleep and when she's unable to do so, she reaches for the half full glass of water sitting on the nightstand and pops a few more pills.

Author:

Ok Charmaine, that should do it, take no more, God has this, and He is going to get you through the difficult days to come. Sleep girl, sleep.

Once heavily sedated, it's not long before her eyelids begin to close. With the overhead light still on and afraid to get up and turn it off, she gives into the medication and drifts off to sleep. There will be no stirring about for her tonight as she now falls asleep safe and sound in the comfort of her own bed.

Chapter Three

A Gift from a Stranger

The following morning and at sun rise Charmaine's peaceful sleep is interrupted way too soon by the alarm on the nightstand. Out of control it blares with a ringing bell noise, ding-a-ling, ding, ding, ding-a-ling it rings and it's a noise that would more than likely wake the dead. It's another day and she is scheduled to work that morning. Poor Charmaine, still drowsy she needs a jolt of caffeine, and quick. Seems the pain meds helped her to sleep but did very little for the aches and pains and the entire trauma she endured last night. Soon she reaches over and gives that little blaring ding-a-ling alarm clock a good slap which lands it face down on the nightstand and immediately the room goes silent. Lying on her back and oh so slowly she turns over to her side, pushes herself up and makes her way to her feet.

Charmaine Prays,

Good Lord, today's going to be a tough day but please help me get through it and most of all Lord, please, please protect me from that evil brute that attacked me last night, Amen, Amen, Amen.

Author:

Well, as expected she is still hurting physically and mentally, and who wouldn't. Hurting from head to toe, and after all of the Amens are said, she would give anything if she could just flop back into bed and hide from the rest of the world with a couple of days to recover. But no can do. There are bills to be paid.

Slowly but surely, she gets dressed and after many attempts to camouflage the scrapes and bruises with makeup, it's time to get going. With all of her clothes dry, she slips on her coat and wraps that unpredictable neck scarf around her neck. Once it's snug, she grabs her slightly smashed handbag and heads out the door locking up behind her. With the pain and cold air lingering, the morning stroll to work isn't going to be a pleasant one. But, lucky for Charmaine in the wee hours of the morning and while she slept, yesterday's cold front blew through headed south and took the rain and blistering wind with it. Yes indeed, it's a beautiful cold sunshiny morning but the warmth from the sun doesn't stop the chitter-chatter sounds coming from her teeth. Also, when she breathes, condensation clouds spew from her mouth and nostrils.

Author:

Doing so, she resembles a mad bull ready to charge attacking anyone or anything that gets in her way.

As she continues on, the plan for today is to take no short cuts but to stay on the original path to and from work. Once she comes upon the alleyway taken last night, there is no stopping, she runs, and runs as fast as she can, desperate to get to work. When she reaches the diner door, she's not only out of breath but the blood flowing through her veins feels as if it were boiling. She is so mad and mostly at herself for allowing herself to be put into such a menacing situation as last night. Well so mad, doesn't really cover how she truly feels because she is more than furious, and most certainly she is worried about his threats but there is one thing she truly feels that she deserves since he stole a freebie from her last night, and that is his name.

Once inside she straps on a clean apron and while storing her coat, scarf and handbag away, this shy introvert is not sure exactly how to go about getting what she now wants. Unsure how to approach others it seems she is going to need a miracle or a possible slip of the tongue from another in the diner. Could she be so lucky? So, with no time to figure out a more detailed plan she can only hope that someone or better yet maybe Bootzy will slip and call him by his given name, not the usual Honey, Darlin' Baby, and Sweetie.

As she heads out of the break room, just the mental thought of working an eight-hour shift with excruciating pain is already taking its toll on her. She begins to regret coming into work and considers whether or not to tell the Boss that she is not feeling good so she can go home. But, with the Boss now standing before her, she has no choice. He hands her a list of her assigned tables and before she can say a word, he rushes off to assist customers at the cash register. Well, so much for that, and as said, a girl's gotta do what she's gotta do, and this appears to be one of those times. With list in hand and a somewhat plan in mind, she sucks it up and hits the floor waiting on her assigned customers.

Throughout the morning and when opportunity allows, she attempts to interrogate as many people as she can, trying to get his name. Unsuccessful, this tough cookie isn't going to give up and with the overwhelming pain starting to get the best of her, she is definitely nervous and maybe terrified is a better word when it comes to seeing the scum ball again. With the morning spent asking questions and watching over her shoulder and not sure that he will appear from out of nowhere, the lunch crowd begins to arrive.

Lucky for Charmaine the scum ball is a no show when his buddy shows up at the diner alone. Within minutes and while Charmaine takes orders from a few feet away the scum ball's buddy has a question for Bootzy. And as you can imagine, Charmaine strains to tune out the noise around her, curious, and anxious to overhear what is being said.

Buddy Asks,
Hey Bootzy, where's your boyfriend, "Fredie J. Rae"?

Bootzy Replies,
No can say… Fredie must have had a wild evening and is probably sleeping it off for all I know.

Once Charmaine hears the name, she flips her order pad and on the back jots down his name, never to forget. Wow, what a blessing from God and she can't believe how fast it took to expose his name.

For days Fredie J. Rae continues to be a no show at the diner. It's as if he disappeared, falling off the face of the earth and for whatever the reason, she doesn't care because all she wants is for him to stay away and leave her alone. And then, few weeks pass when Charmaine meanders from out of the kitchen balancing a large tray of food overhead and much to her surprise… "Just guess what the cat drug in"?

Author:
If you said Fredie J. Rae "Mr. Scum Ball," you're right.

Yep, after being a no-show for several weeks, he's back and there he sits in his usual spot at the bar flirting with his favorite waitress, Bootzy. Charmaine is shocked by his presence and can't believe that he had the nerve to show his face after what he did. Within seconds she stumbles over a small rubber mat almost sending food and tray flying right into the laps of many customers. With the wobbly tray now sitting on a nearby stand she tries to control her shaking hands while serving folks. It seems Bootzy, Fredie J. Rae, and a few others caught a glimpse of the almost disaster. With all eyes now focused on her they all laugh as if it was the funniest thing they'd ever seen.

Author:
Now embarrassed, there is no doubt in Charmaine's mind that Bootzy and Fredie J. Rae would have loved seeing her hit the floor landing on her keister and sending the food flying.

Well by George, that day was definitely a tough one and as tough as it was, she survived and moved forward concentrating on her job and not the few jerks that would surround her at times. The next morning and approximately one month after the rape, Charmaine finds herself on her knees nauseated, heaving, and hugging the toilet. She believes that she has the flu but, when the morning symptoms continue throughout the week, she realizes that her menstrual cycle is also late and she panics.

Charmaine Reacts,
Oh no, this can't be happening, please don't be true, pregnant and by that scum ball, I can't take this, It can't be, It can't be, It can't be true.

Within days the symptoms go away, she's feeling better and it seems she may have assumed the worse way too soon, and now anxiously awaits her next cycle to begin.

Author:
You may be asking, with her past lifestyle how did she not

get pregnant before? Well, it seems her lowlife parents took care of that issue, with birth control pills always on hand, and faithfully they made sure a pill slid down her throat daily.

When she escaped from Little Wicked, she never dreamed that she would ever need them since her new lifestyle wasn't going to include sexual intercourse for a long time. So, with one menstrual cycle missed and as she anxiously waits for another, unfortunately it doesn't come, and she is with child. This unwanted gift from a stranger is now a reality and the timing has just become one of her worst nightmares.

Unfortunately, the evil Fredie J. Rae has now left her pregnant, scarred forever, and not to mention any and all plans for the future, destroyed and with all now tossed to the curbside. Charmaine spends several sleepless nights tormenting herself, wishing over and over that she could undo that spontaneous decision. Unable to do so, she now struggles with the reality of what lies ahead and even has thoughts of an abortion. Well, those thoughts are quickly eliminated removed from her mind since she is a faithful believer in God and pro-life.

Sure, Charmaine's life hasn't been easy but taking an unborn baby's life would be way too much for her already damaged soul and conscience to handle. With new plans on the horizon, she seeks help from a local Catholic home for unwed mothers. But one thing stands in her way: the home is at full occupancy, so they add her name to a waiting list, anticipating a two month wait or less.

In the meantime, and not liking it at all, Charmaine continues to work at the diner. The stress of waiting for the home to call is overwhelming, she is miserable physically, and mentally. She does her best to disguise the little baby bump now bulging slightly from behind her apron. With the weight gain, bloating, and having to walk to and from work and being on her feet all day... the worst part is having to watch Bootzy and Fredie J. Rae flirting and carrying on amongst themselves.

The call from the home needs to come and come fast because the intimidation, harassment, and in-your-face attitudes aren't easy to deal with, especially when one's pregnant. With poor Charmaine getting more than her fair share of harassment and intimidation she is pretty much at the end of her rope and teeters with the thought of calling the cops anyway. She'd love to see handcuffs slapped on baby daddy, and Bootzy's face as they haul his disgusting keister away to jail.

Author:

I guarantee, as arrogant as he is, I'm sure he wouldn't make a good jail bird.

The days, hours, and minutes seem to move at a snail's pace, and then finally, out of the blue the awaited call comes from the home and it is time to move on.

Author:

Oh yes indeed, she is definitely ready, it's time to move on, quit as soon as possible and do it before the Boss, co-workers and most of all Fredie J. Rae can learn that she is with child.

For some time now Charmaine has made the pregnancy her very own secret, and hers alone, and if she can help it, there will be no baby daddy interference allowed… "PERIOD!"

Within days Charmaine quits her job and then moves into the home for unwed mothers, and there she will stay until her baby is born. At the home she finds refuge in her surroundings and with no more worries, she is safe and protected from the gossip and the evil brute who raped her. Soon she falls into a depressed and withdrawn state of mind, determined to stay in her room as much as possible.

Very seldom does she participate in the group sessions where everyone shares their story, and with most being much younger, she is just not there yet. Indeed, and with all things considered, being the oldest she's ashamed and embarrassed to open up to total strangers. Her shyness plays a big part in keeping her at bay. When a few weeks go by, the homes Superior Nun pays her a visit. Her name is Frances May Elliott, and many call her Frances May. Quickly, their friendship blossoms and this is exactly what Charmaine needs with her pregnancy becoming a difficult one. Frances May dedicates many hours visiting, helping her, and praying that Charmaine will eventually reach out and share her story.

Soon, her due date which was Sunday October 15, 1972 has come and gone. Totally ready to get this baby out, she becomes extremely anxious, scared, and overwhelmed with emotions. She also continues not to participate in any and all home activities. With the baby refusing to be born she isolates herself in her room.

Then, on October 29th, all of Charmaine's secrets become almost too much to bear, weighing heavily on her heart, and finally the time comes, she needs to talk to someone. It seems all of Frances May's patience has finally paid off. Charmaine is ready to open up and share her story—with Frances May, and her alone. She needs a shoulder to cry on and Frances May is the only one she feels she can trust.

After she requests a visit from Frances May, within minutes she comes to her side. Frances May sits silently beside her on the bed and finally Charmaine's heartfelt story is told. Sobbing with her face cupped in her hands she begins with her past…

First, she begins with Little Wicked, Texas tucked away in West Texas and almost invisible to the eye, her upbringing, her escape, and then the rape in Corpus Christi. Trying to hold back her tears, Frances May continues to sit in silence, shocked at what this woman has gone through and continues to go through. In-between sniffles Charmaine focuses mainly on the rape and what led up to it, the trauma, the threats, and most important the rapist name, Fredie J. Rae. Soon after she mentions his name she regrets doing so. She truly believes that the scum ball will do what he threatened so she pleads with Frances May to never reveal his name to anyone. She becomes delirious thinking that they both could be in danger now. Frances May comforts her and compassionately vows to never tell another soul.

Frances May Says,

Charmaine, your secret is safe with me, I promise.

The next day, and early in the morning a promising sign comes, Charmaine's water breaks and she goes into labor. She is rushed to a nearby hospital located on Ocean Drive. Once again, Frances May is at her side and refuses to leave with the labor pains intense and continuing into the night.

Then on Tuesday October 31st and at 8:46 am Charmaine delivers a baby girl with Frances May observing from across the room. The routine is pretty much normal in the labor room once the baby arrives. But, with baby not breathing, the doctor holds her up by her feet and slaps her little behind as she sucks in her first breath of air. Like babies before her, the little toot didn't like that slap to her behind and it seems her lungs are working just fine as she screams out bloody murder.

The baby crying brings a huge smile to Charmaine's face but not for long because within minutes of delivering, there are complications...

Charmaine's heart begins to go straight line on a nearby monitor; she's going into cardiac arrest. With no time to waste one nurse wraps the screaming baby into a blanket and then hands her over to Frances May while the doctor and head nurse administers CPR to Charmaine. In a matter of seconds, the room went from a joyful routine to utter chaos. Then twenty-two minutes thirty-six seconds later and while Frances May comforts the crying baby, the doctor pronounces Charmaine expired and documents the time of death at 9:10 am.

Frances May Calls out,
Oh my goodness, what is happening?

Never expecting Charmaine to die, the obvious unfolds before her eyes and with not one word said, a nurse tenderly drapes a white sheet over Charmaine's face, and during all of the drama Charmaine's baby girl has finally cried herself to sleep. With the baby safe and secure in Frances May's arms she can't believe Charmaine is gone and tearfully asks for a little private time with Charmaine and her baby girl. Her request is granted. Still lying on the delivery table Frances May stands at her side, she mourns over Charmaine and can't believe that the Lord has just taken her from such a joyful moment in her life. So sad...

Indeed, and as sad as it may be, Charmaine will never ever lay eyes upon her precious little baby girl and as true as that may be, Frances May decides to give Charmaine's little baby girl a moment to bond with her mother. She removes the sheet from Charmaine's body. Her breasts are bare with her gown ripped open after having CPR administered. While the baby sleeps, Frances May gently unwraps the blanket which is now stained with afterbirth. Trying not to wake the baby, she carefully places her naked little body atop of her Mama's bosom and there they both lay, flesh to flesh, and chest to chest. When the baby starts to fuss and squirm Frances May places Charmaine's hands over her back and soon she nestles her little head into her Mama's bosom sighing, content and bonding with the mother she'll never know.

Frances May Says as her hand caresses Charmaine's forehead,

Charmaine, meet your precious little baby girl. This is my promise to you my sweet friend, I will personally see that your little bundle of joy will be placed into a loving Christian God-Fearing home and your baby daddy will never know of her existence, as I promised before.

Soon, the head nurse returns and it's time to address the baby's needs. Frances May removes the baby from Charmaine's bosom and then covers her smiling face one last time. Again, the baby is not happy, screaming at the top of her lungs. Frances May quickly bundles her up tightly into her blanket and before she hands her over to the nurse, she gives her a sweet little kiss on the cheek.

Frances May Says,

Ok Baby Girl, this kiss is from your birth mother, the mother you'll never know, I promise, I'll see you soon.

Sad and in mourning, Frances May returns to the home and there she spends most of the night crying as she prays for Charmaine's soul and her precious little baby girl. Due to Charmaine's sudden death her baby spends a couple of days in the hospital nursery being carefully monitored. When a few days pass and with no signs of health issues, it is decided that she be released to an adoption agency. This was decided since the birth certificate showed no other relatives and Father listed as unknown and nowhere to be found. Since Frances May is the Superior Nun at the home where Charmaine lived and was present during the delivery the hospital lets her know immediately. She jumps into her car and heads for the adoption agency and hopes to keep all of the promises made to Charmaine. She meets with a Mrs. Anderson the director/caseworker at the agency and before Frances May can make all of her demands known, Mrs. Anderson interrupts her…

Mrs. Anderson Says,

Miss Frances, I need you to glance over my right shoulder.

Do you see the couple in the next room holding a baby wrapped in a pink blanket?

Frances May Says,

Yes, is that Charmaine's baby their holding?

Mrs. Anderson Says,

Yes, and today they have become her parents. Now, please allow me to explain... The couple (Dr. Russell Leland Dawalt and his wife Catherine) are a typical all-American family, frugal, not extravagant, and meet most and if not all of your demands. God-fearing Christians, not Catholic but Church of Christ, married for twenty years, living and educated in Austin, Texas. They are more than able to provide for the baby and their two biological boys Rick ten and Larry (Bubba) eight. Then she explains their reasons for adopting. Since the birth of their last son Catherine is no longer able to have children so they decided to complete their family by adopting a newborn baby girl. For several years they have been waiting for this moment and Charmaine's baby seemed to be a perfect fit for their needs.

Mrs. Anderson Asks?

Miss Frances would you like to meet and spend some time with them before they all go back home to Austin.

Frances May Says,

Yes please... I have a few things I'd like to share with them if that's ok?

Mrs. Anderson Says,

Indeed, please follow me and I'll introduce you to the Dawalt's and their beautiful baby girl, Cassie Lynn Dawalt.

Frances May spends close to an hour with the Dawalt's and during that time they allow her to hold baby Cassie Lynn, and of course Frances May is so thrilled to do so. While they visit baby Cassie Lynn sleeps. This gives Frances May an opportunity to share the heartfelt story about Charmaine. She shares everything stopping short of the Father's name. Tearfully shaken by what they heard when Frances May finishes, they ask if she knows the Fathers name and if he could be a threat to them. Frances May tells them yes, that she knows his name, but assures them that he shouldn't be a threat since his name is not on the birth certificate and the baby's mother insisted that it never be known. Shortly after confessing to knowing his name she explains her reason for not sharing that bit of information with them.

Frances May Says,
There are times when secrets or promises are meant to be kept and this happens to be one of those times. I hope you understand.

With the baby stirring about and under the circumstances the Dawalt's do not pursue the issue as they are anxious to wrap up things and take their baby girl back to Austin. It's time to get baby Cassie Lynn home so she can meet her two brothers. So, the Dawalt's scramble gathering up all documents and baby items needed for the trip. Frances May is happy for them and at the same time she is sad. With everything happening so fast she realizes that she'll never see them again and reconsiders whether or not to break that one promise made to Charmaine. Since Charmaine is deceased Frances May decides that she needs to do what's right for all involved, so she walks them to their car and one last time gives Charmaine's baby girl one last kiss on the cheek.

Frances May Says,
Goodbye Cassie Lynn Dawalt… May God always bless you and give you a wonderful life with your parents.

Doctor Dawalt jumps into the driver's seat while Catherine sitting nearby holds baby Cassie Lynn. Frances May taps on the window and when Catherine rolls down the window, she slips her a tiny tightly folded piece of paper.

Frances May Says,
For whatever reason one day you may need to know what's written inside. So, please keep this in a safe place and never share with another.

Immediately, Frances May turns around, with head down and somewhat disappointed with herself she shamefully walks away never to see them again. With baby Cassie Lynn becoming fussy Catherine slips the paper into her purse and the Dawalt family drives off into the sunset.

Chapter Four

Growing Up Dawalt in Austin, Texas

The Dawalts and baby Cassie Lynn, head down I-37 towards the Corpus Christi International Airport where they take the next plane home to Austin. As the pilot taxies towards the runway and while he waits for his turn to lift off the Dawalt's curiosity gets the best of them. What is written on the tightly folded piece of paper? Dad holds baby Cassie Lynn while Mom opens it, and there it is, nothing more just Cassie Lynn's biological Fathers name, "Fredie J. Rae." This will be one name neither will forget.

Catherine quickly shoves the paper back into her purse, choosing not to focus on "Fredie J. Rae" but the joyful moments with baby Cassie Lynn. Once home, they find scattered throughout the yard and house all kinds of pink ribbons, balloons, and signs that scream out, "Welcome home, Cassie Lynn."

It is a big celebration for the new addition into the family and with the welcome mat all laid out, some family members have already arrived, and others mingle in later. When her two brothers meet her at the door it is a heartwarming moment as they can't seem to get enough of her. If one's not holding her the other one is. Throughout the day family and friends come and go except for one uncle who hangs around for a few days before returning to Houston.

His name is Randy Dawalt, an entrepreneur and wealthy oil tycoon in Houston Texas and he is Doctor Dawalt's older brother. Unlike his younger brother, he is unmarried and with no children of his own. This makes him the favorite uncle many wished they had when growing up. So, with that said Uncle Randy loves spending his fortune and over the years his two nephews have always been the center of his generosity and now it's baby Cassie Lynn's turn. When Uncle Randy finally gets his turn to hold her, all it takes is one look into her eyes and precious little face and the little toot has him at hook, line and sinker. He thinks she is the most beautiful baby he has ever seen. Years would pass with family birthday parties, vacations, church and holiday get-togethers, elementary, middle and high school graduations, first kiss, boyfriends, and not to exclude all of life's struggles, heartaches, and a few secrets.

But, before many of those things happen and at age six, one day curious Cassie Lynn has a question for her parents. With a house full of brunets, she wants to know why she is the only blonde in the family. Caught off guard Mom and Dad aren't expecting a question like that at such a young age. But, as unexpected as it was, it seems it's time to tell her that she is adopted. So, they sit her down and share limited details of course. They explain how she was a blessing from God and how lucky they were to have her as their daughter. Well, being six and as expected she takes it well, and when it comes to her parents' explanation, her little face lights up with a big smile and as usual she continues on with her life, playing and doing what most little girls do. At age six, sharing limited details is a good idea, and when or if other details are ever needed, doing so will need to happen at a more appropriate age.

Moving forward, and years later, Cassie Lynn longs to learn more about why she was adopted. She becomes anxious for more information and when she turns eighteen her parents finally share her birth mother's heartfelt story. Although she is of age, they choose to withhold such things like being conceived during rape and her biological father's name, sparing her those crucial details. As difficult as the story is to hear, Cassie Lynn is embarrassed after learning what her biological grandparents did to her birth mother. Cassie Lynn even acknowledges, that not even her rebellious years can compare to what her birth mother went through and she is so thankful that she was placed into such a loving family. With more information now out in the open, Cassie Lynn totally drops the subject and chooses to never speak again about her horrible biological family.

It is May 1992 and a twenty-year-old Cassie Lynn Dawalt is graduating from college, "The University of Texas." Now, with a Business Degree in Management in hand, it's time to benefit from the rewards of a good education. A few weeks before the big graduation ceremony she has a job interview with an up and growing refinery off I-37 and in of all towns, Corpus Christi. With her being so young the company is hesitant on hiring her, but when they see the 4.0 average, that's the icing on the cake and she lands a purchasing agent's position which she will start on Wednesday July 1st. The job at the refinery has its advantages, even opportunities to advance, and will allow her to pay her bills and more. Indeed, it sure beats flipping burgers for all of those years in college. Unknown to her adopted family, and after hearing her birthmother's story a few years ago, the need to learn more about her birth mother is stronger than ever. So, as you might have guessed Cassie Lynn's parents, family, and a current somewhat boyfriend aren't so happy about the upcoming move. But, after many attempts to change her mind her parents finally give up since she is an adult and capable of making her own decisions. Within days Cassie Lynn breaks up with that current somewhat boyfriend and he is devastated since he had wedding bells in mind for their future. His vision for the future was them married, her barefoot and pregnant, and raising a hand full of kids. Well, not so fast friend, Cassie Lynn isn't ready for marriage and a house full of kids, she wants a career, and nothing or anyone is going to get in her way. Oh, and one more thing… she doesn't even like going barefooted.

Author:
Ouch! Someone got'a Kleenex.

With all of the goodbyes said to immediate family and friends and on the first Saturday in June she finds herself up at the crack of dawn. Mom and Dad are up to, as they help her pack up all of her worldly possessions into her little white 1988 Camry which was a high school graduation gift from her Uncle Randy. Yes indeed, who would of thunk so much girlie stuff could fit into that little white four-door Camry, but it does.

So, with the car tightly packed and the trunk bulging, Mom and Dad are within minutes of becoming "Empty Nesters." Their sweet little Cassie Lynn is the last of three children to graduate from college and move away. Happy and sad tears begin to flow, she's within minutes of leaving, and when they become unstoppable, she jumps in her car and pulls out of the driveway.

Mom is bawling her head off and Dad waves goodbye as she gives a little toot on the horn waving goodbye, and eventually disappears from their site. As tearful as the moment is the "Empty Nesters" couldn't be prouder. Cassie Lynn drives through town, and at the same time she wipes away a few lingering tears from her face.

She's going to miss her parents but at the moment she is overwhelmed with excitement as she begins her new journey as an "Independent" woman.

Dodging traffic, she tries to avoid colliding with speeders as she drives south on I-10 eventually making a detour over to I-59. Once on I-59 she heads south to Victoria, Texas for lunch. You may ask, why the detour and lunch in Victoria? The plan is to meet her Uncle Randy and celebrate her new job over a big juicy T-bone steak and before going on to Corpus Christi. The best part about this lunch date is, he's buying. After a nice visit with her favorite Uncle and scarfing down the T-bone steak she's back on I-59 and heading south to her final destination, Corpus Christi.

With not much daylight remaining, the sun begins to set, and as darkness creeps into the endless sky, from Victoria she's looking at a two-hour possibly two-and-a-half-hour drive with maybe a few extra pit stops if needed. Well, the first stop comes shortly after leaving Victoria when the windshield wiper fluid goes dry due to a pesky little bug. It's the Plecia Nearctica bug (AKA: two by two, honeymoon flies, love bugs) and they are flying in clusters, swarming, and attacking every windshield and front bumper on the road.

With a little elbow grease, she manages to get most of them off while she caps off her gas tank at the same time. To quench her thirst, she buys a diet drink and then hits the road again. Soon, and after several gulps, the cruise control is set and with the sun teetering on the horizon blaring in her eyes, she slides her sunglasses (sexy specs), back on which hang from the overhead visor above. So, with her tank full of gas, and a nice cool drink in hand it's time to crank up the radio and find an oldies radio station to listen too. Oh yeah, she is now rockin' and singing, off key and who cares, as she makes her way down I-59.

Dusk covers the sky as she makes her way into Refugio Texas. Slowly, she creeps into town and as she makes her way through, she witnesses a few folks being stopped, assuming they were speeding and getting a ticket. If there is one thing she doesn't want it is a ticket, because her squeaky clean record is how she keeps her insurance premiums down and at her age that's the way she likes it. With flashing lights in her rearview mirror, she continues to drive at a snail's pace, nice and easy as she lets up even more on the accelerator. Thank goodness, soon the patrol car goes past and they're not after her, she drives on cautiously and keeps a close eye on her speedometer. Carefully she maintains the thirty-five mile an hour speed limit and manages to get through town with no ticket, and then it's on to Bayside and Portland. Well, that little thirty-five-minute drive from Refugio to Portland didn't take long with Portland now in her rearview mirror as she's cruisin' over the "Causeway" bridge in-between Portland and North Beach.

She is in awe, excited by what she sees ahead—and unaware of the dangers that await.

Cassie Lynn Says,

"Wow!" What a sight for sore eyes, finally, Corpus Christi Texas, my hometown.

With a few cars lingering about, she's got a sassy attitude going when she yell's out…

"Move out of the way folks. Yours truly, Cassie Lynn has arrived!"

Wow is right, it's a clear night with the Corpus Christi sky and the surrounding areas engulfed with thousands maybe millions of sparkling lights.

Author:

Here's a little trivia, Corpus Christi also referred to as "The Sparkling City by the Sea" and defined as the feast of "The Body of Christ."

The city lights are absolutely breathtaking when Cassie reaches the top of the Harbor Bridge. Maneuvering her little Camry at slow pace, she is awestruck by the view and keeps a close eye on the exit signs wanting to stay in the downtown area. Lucky for her within minutes she's on Shoreline Dr. where she passes several motel-hotels and eventually comes upon a hospital, it's Spohn Hospital a name she's familiar with and where she was born. Directly across from the hospital is a nice Inn, it looks safe, so she checks in, beds down for the night with plans of staying a few days until she can find a permanent place to live. With it getting late and as promised she calls Mom and Dad and as most parents they're up and waiting, ready to say, "You made it." Well, after a few commute details, Mom is still a little teary eyed about the move and can't seem to shake off the sniffles.

Tired and ready to unwind, Cassie reassures them that she is going to be fine. Before hanging up she agrees to touch base in a few days and tries to ease their worries. More mature than others her age she tells them, life is good and suggests that they focus on her new journey and the adventure and excitement of it all. Soon, she unpacks her suitcase and being a perfectionist, she neatly hangs most items and places other personal items in dresser drawers. Once everything is in its place, she slips into her PJs, grabs the television remote, flops into an easy chair and begins to search for something interesting to watch. Distracted by the lights across the bay there she sits "Little Miss Independent" with no more parents looking over her shoulder and telling her what to do, when to come or be home, hit the books and get to bed you have class in the morning. Yippee, I'm finally my own Boss and with that thought she starts to feel bad knowing that she has made her parents sad, moving from Austin. Now somewhat regretful, she wishes she had only cut the cord sooner than later, attending college elsewhere in the country.

Author:

So, how does one cut the cord from hovering parents? Well, like Cassie Lynn, have a plan in place, calmly and firmly stand your ground showing your parents and others that you've got this, you're now educated and totally capable of working and providing for yourself.

Four days later she discovers the perfect apartment on the outskirts of town, near the Flour Bluff area, newly built, a one bedroom furnished with washer and dryer. She chooses an apartment on the second floor for its attic storage room and because as a single woman she feels safer on the second floor. She moves in immediately wanting to shop and have everything in its place before starting her job on Wednesday July 1st. After being raised in a frugal household she manages to get groceries bought and a little shopping done while staying within her budget. By Tuesday evening she finally plops down on the bluish teal brocade sofa. She's pooped. The dishes are washed and stacked in the kitchen cabinets, the bedroom and closet items are organized with a few girlie keepsakes stored in the hall walk-in attic. She is totally thankful for that little extra space. As she relaxes, she admires the new sweet little beach scene which hangs over the dining room table and like a magnet her thoughts drift to tomorrow and her first day at work. Soon startled, the phone jars her thoughts back to the present. It's another call from her parents calling to say how proud they are and want to wish her good luck tomorrow.

Parents Ask,
Tomorrows a big day Darl'an, are you nervous?

Cassie Lynn Answers,
Well, maybe a little… I'm starting to have a few first-day jitters and wish I felt as confident as I sound. But, not to worry folks by morning I plan to walk into work with my head up high and get to work striving to keep the plant running and make the boss look good. How's that sound Dad?

Dad Says,
Sweet Girl couldn't have said it better if I had said it myself.

After a short conversation with her parents, she slips her "Tweety Bird" night shirt on over her head, giggling at the thought of a powerful purchasing agent decked out in teenager's attire. I wonder, maybe soon something more mature is in the future? Before crashing for the night it's time to lay out tomorrow's wardrobe attire, the newly purchased emerald green suit with pearl buttons, and two inch camel-colored pumps that also match a new camel-colored leather attaché case. After all is laid out, she saunters back to the kitchen for a small glass of apple juice, sighs as she sets her alarm for 5:30 am. Like some folks and before she gets cozy into bed, she checks the alarm one last time assuring herself that it is set to go off. Finally, it's time to count sheep.

Author:
Well, over the moon they go, one, two, three, ok, maybe at her age not so funny but, I wonder could there possibly be some adults in the world who never stop counting sheep and continue to do this childhood remedy before falling asleep? Nah!

As she lies there in the dark, not counting sheep and all snuggled under the covers, a dim light shone through the bedroom mini blinds. The light was not enough to keep her from falling asleep or awake but just enough for her to see her way around the apartment without turning on a light. Seems little “Miss Independent” isn’t quite comfortable staying by herself since there’s always been someone stirring about in another room. Snuggled comfortably on her side with the covers pulled up tucked under her chin, her eyes are focused on the bedroom door until she drifts off to sleep.

Before dawn, Cassie Lynn awakes from a deep sleep and is aware of a strange but sad feeling that envelops her entire body. Groggy she glances over to the nightstand. The big red numbers on the clock faithfully shine in the dark, 2:30 am… with still a little more time for sleep before the alarm goes off. Then, all of the sudden a loud “BOOM!” shatters the stillness in the night and puts her in a do not move, frozen position.

It sounded as if something had hit the wall right above the headboard. Flipping on her back and not moving her head, wide-eyed she scans all corners of the room, but nothing moves. She stares at the door, and swallows all of the accumulated spit which swished about in her mouth. Somewhat convinced and assuming she is alone in the apartment she believes that the loud thump more than likely originated from her neighbor’s apartment next door. Next, something unexpected happens, out of the blue a faint cry can be heard from next door and it’s obvious it’s not a child or woman, it’s a man crying. His sad cry keeps her from falling back to sleep so she just lies there listening and wonders how much longer he will keep her awake. For a half hour or more the weeping continues when it becomes difficult to hold her eyelids open. But soon silence blankets the night once more and no need to count sheep when she drifts right off into a deep sleep. After a restless night, and at 5:30 am the noisy alarm announces its time to get up and get going.

Chapter Five

Independent and Striving for Success

Groggily, Cassie Lynn hits the sleep button, desperate for five more minutes of sleep, she hits it again, and finally at 5:40 am she swings her feet onto the floor. She stretches a bit and then sluggishly marches her way to the kitchen to plug in the coffee pot. Between sips of coffee she dabs on a little foundation and eye makeup; styling her long blonde hair with a curling iron; and then steps into the new emerald green suit with pearl buttons.

You see, unlike her biological birth mother Charmaine Rene Davis who had a homely look, tall 5'8" in stature, slender, and well-endowed, Cassie Lynn is slightly the opposite with some resemblances such as slender, blonde hair and olive tone skin. Cassie Lynn on the other hand when barefoot stands 5'5", petite, not as busty as her birth mother, and obviously she inherited her beautiful facial features from some unknown relative. Lucky girl, as she needs very little makeup to offset her beauty. Oh yes indeed, the emerald green suit with pearl buttons on the long sleeves and accenting the front of the jacket already had sold written all over it and before she ever laid eyes on it. Some girls like their diamonds but Cassie Lynn loves her pearls. Setting on the bed to put on her two-inch camel-colored pumps she glances into the mirror. She smiles and notices that the suit color complements her hazel eyes and the pumps match her olive tone skin. When she purchased the pumps and standing at 5'5", she considered going with high heels but reconsidered from a physical point of view; she made the right decision; the pumps have the physical and professional look she sought. The mirror not only revealed a young but professional look, but it reminded her that the degree and knowledge in-between her ears will certainly accomplish all of the success that she strives for. With one last glance into the mirror she admires herself from all angles and soon a sassy attitude is revealed.

Cassie Lynn Crows,

"Yes, yes, and yes Girlfriend you look good." Stand up straight, don't slouch and by all means act confident and go show others what you got.

Absolutely, it is called confidence, and this gal has got it. She straightens the seams of her skirt, grabs her keys, attaché case, and strides to the door. It's now 7:05 am and still plenty of time to get to work. Closing and locking the door behind her, she checks twice making sure it is locked and shut tight. That's one habit she was taught at an early age and promised a few family members that she would continue to do, and faithfully. The commute to work is great with traffic moving smoothly with no problems. The sun shines brightly with partly cloudy skies and a little on the breezy side with temp in the low 80's. God has blessed her and what more could a person want. One more glance at her watch. It's 7:35 am when she approaches the refinery. Right on schedule. She stops at the guard gate and as she fumbles to get the car window down the guard smiles as he patiently waits.

Guard Asks,

Good morning Miss, what can I do for you?

Cassie Lynn Says,

Good Morning I'm Cassie Lynn Dawalt a new employee for the purchasing department.

Guard Asks, as he checks a new employee clipboard revealing her name.

Your first day I assume?

Cassie Lynn Replies,

Yes Sir, I need to know the procedure for parking could you possibly help me out?

With vehicles now lining up behind hers, the guard with the name tag Dutch Allen, very politely instructs her to a designated parking area for all administrative employees, but before driving away he taps on her windshield advising that she immediately get the required parking sticker needed from the HR (Human Resources) department. Once parked, she first reports to her Boss "Procurement Manager" Preston Erwin and from there it is on to HR to fill out all of the necessary paperwork, W2, 401K, insurance information, and etc., and most of all get that much-needed parking sticker as required by the guard.

After walking into the HR department Cassie Lynn is approached by a woman slightly smaller than herself. The teensy-weensy little woman is wearing some of the most beautiful stiletto high heels that she has ever seen, black patent and with gold tips. She appears to be in her mid to late thirties and a very attractive woman, her shoulder length brown hair perfectly combed, make-up applied with no smudges and her black pin-striped pantsuit neatly draped to her body. As for those stilettos, Ooh-la-la, they complement her outfit perfectly. Before Cassie Lynn can finish her full name, the woman smiles, introduces herself as Juliana Gilmore. She is the "Human Resources Manager" who was on vacation and detained while out of the country during Cassie Lynn's April interview and hiring.

Juliana Gilmore Says, while shaking Cassie Lynn's hand,

Oh let me guess, you must be Cassie Dawalt and you're the new purchasing agent Preston Erwin hired when I was on vacation, right?

Cassie Lynn Replies,

Yes Ma'am, and I need to fill out some paperwork and get my parking sticker for my car… Ma'am I also prefer to be called Cassie Lynn if you don't mind.

Juliana Gilmore Says, with a somewhat cocky smirky tone,

Oh absolutely, and you can drop the Ma'am when answering my questions. Call me Juliana, "You got it!"

Whoops, oh my, oh my, Cassie Lynn, it's only an hour and a half into arriving and you have already put your foot into your mouth. Well, it seems she insulted Juliana and is unsure what she said exactly. Cassie Lynn chooses not to respond when Juliana apologizes and not for the snippy remark but because her Secretary Maxine Kullman is running late, and she needed to be in a managers' meeting ten minutes ago. As Juliana escorts Cassie Lynn to the door and before she scurries down the hallway to her meeting, it's agreed that Cassie Lynn will return at 11:00 am to take care of the necessary paperwork. Back in purchasing and before getting settled in her office the Boss assigns Jayleen Green, the only senior purchasing agent in the office to give Cassie Lynn a quick tour of the building and department locations. Finally, the time has come to see her office. The first thing that catches her eye is the engraved name plate on the oak desk revealing her name and position, one personal computer atop, and behind the desk a black leather chair, one book shelf stuffed with vendor catalogs and for privacy a small framed window on the door with mounted mini-blinds. With plenty of room on the bare walls, it seems there is plenty of room to display her newly framed degree. Talk about feeling like little "Miss Big Shot," she pushes the door slightly ajar and then kicks back in her chair and swings those cute little pumps onto the corner of the desk. While smiling and as she looks about, she begins to feel as if she has just won the lottery, and out of the blue and without warning, the door swings open.

Jayleen Green Says,
Ok, "Little Miss Big Shot" time to get to work.

Cassie Lynn Wonders,
Hum, how in the world did she know what I was thinking?

With both giggling, Jayleen flops down on the desk a two-inch pile of purchase orders and reminds her about her 11:00 meeting with HR and insists that she not be late. With her feet back on the ground she has thirty minutes left on the clock to scan through some of the paperwork and before making that appointment.

Well, it seems Cassie Lynn doesn't take Jayleen's advice, showing up eight minutes late as she stands in front of the HR Secretary's desk. An older woman sits behind the desk and while on the phone she frowns as she looks over her dark rimmed glasses at her. Then she glances up at a clock on the wall and it's clear her lips are saying, you're late.

Author:

Way to go Cassie Lynn, earlier you not only made one other person in HR upset, but now two.

The woman points her down to a chair nearby while she finishes with her call. Cassie Lynn presumes the woman on the phone is Maxine Kullman when she notices a name plate on the desk. While she waits and as she listens to her conversation, she notices that the woman has a funny and bubbly personality and those thick dark rimmed glasses that she wears on the tip of her nose just add to her personality. Then, in passing someone peeks in the door giving a friendly shout out to the woman on the phone, calling her Maxine, which definitely confirms who she is. Maxine pretty much resembles someone's grandmother by the pictures on the desk. She's an older woman, some would say grandmother, with gray roots fading throughout her auburn hair, and high rosy cheekbones and wearing just a smidgeon of red rouge to make her face look thinner. The more she listens to Maxine talk, it's for certain she is a real hoot and hopes she's not too angry at her for being late. Shortly and after Maxine is off the phone it's obvious that she is not, or has forgotten, because she flops several forms in front of Cassie Lynn to fill out. Once all forms needed for employment are completed, Cassie Lynn waits for security to bring her much needed parking sticker for her car, and photo ID badge which she intends to wear on the bottom seam of her suit jacket.

While waiting for security to show up, she and Maxine share in a little small talk when Juliana makes a mad dash into the room. The woman doesn't even say a word and just goes directly to her office. She is in a hurry and who knew someone could walk so fast in stilettos? Some would say, how rude was that, but not so fast someone follows behind her, and it is Dion Martine Juliana's ex-boyfriend. Dion Martine certainly surpasses the saying, "full package." He is young, six-foot-tall, dark and handsome, big brown eyes, jet black hair combed back like a gangster, and dressed in a neatly pressed casual white shirt and khaki pants.

Author:

Dion Martine, a masculine name with what seems to be a

French, Italian, possibly African descent. Yes indeed, quiet the luscious name as it rolls off the tongue and no doubt about it, God worked overtime when he made this guy.

As Dion makes his way to Juliana's office, he makes a quick stop along the way to chit chat with Maxine, and he is curious who the little blonde is wearing the eye-catching, emerald-green suit with pearls. Sure, Maxine may be up in years but she ain't dead, and it is obvious she likes seeing this guy as she jumps up from her seat and begins to make small talk with him. Within seconds, those dark rimmed glasses are atop her head, grinning, just totally starstruck, and giddy like a little teenager. A few minutes into the conversation Maxine can't seem to keep Dion's attention as he is focused on one thing and that's the gal in the emerald-green suit. Not knowing who he is Cassie Lynn tries to ignore his uncomfortable glances wishing security would show up and show up quick. Like a genie, wish granted, when security walks through the door with her ID badge and sticker. While she clips it to the bottom seam of her suit jacket, Juliana reappears, and she is not happy when she finds Dion hanging around Maxine's desk laughing and carrying on with her and assuming, Cassie Lynn too. Immediately, she picks up on the flirtatious attraction between Dion and Cassie Lynn.

Juliana Says, as she clamps on and cuddles Dion's arm,
Hi babe, I'm starved. Maxine I'm going to lunch, be back soon…

Dion Says, with his eyes zoomed in on Cassie Lynn's ID badge,
Nice to meet you "Purchasing Agent" Cassie Lynn Dawalt, maybe I'll see you again sometime?

Aware of Juliana's and Dion's past, Maxine slips back into her seat, slides those dark rimmed glasses back down to the tip of her nose and believes that a cat fight is about to happen. Well not today Maxine. Juliana wouldn't stoop that low, but she is a smooth operator, and there is no way she's going to let some new employee move in on what she considers to be hers. Arm and arm she quickly drags Dion out the door and off for a bite to eat.

Cassie Lynn Asks Maxine,
What a cute couple, are they married?

Maxine Says as she cracks up laughing,
Heavens no, at the moment Dion Martine is an ex-boyfriend of Juliana's… They have an on and off again cougar and young stud relationship and neither has been married.

Cassie Lynn Asks,
Wow, how old are they?

Maxine Says,
He is twenty-nine and out of respect for Juliana I'll just say, mid-thirties. You know I noticed the attraction between you and Dion, are you interested?

Cassie Lynn Says.
No, just curious.

The phone rings and it's a perfect opportunity to escape from all of Maxine's questions, and with no time to go out for lunch, she heads down the hall to the vending machines. With a diet drink and snack in hand she makes a mad dash back to her office.

With way too much time spent in HR, and while away, Jayleen managed to slip a few more purchase orders into the pile left on Cassie Lynn's desk earlier. In-between sips of diet cola and crunching on salt and vinegar chips, her salty fingertips race about the computer keyboard trying to input as much pertinent information as possible. With the morning somewhat wasted she's behind and needs to get caught up before five o'clock. As she types away she's not the least bit worried because not only did she graduate from college with a 4.0 average but she was also one of the fastest typist at UT. The keyboard is smokin' but not for long when her mind begins to drift to guess who, Dion Martine.

Author:
Come on, what's up with that, she's just five hours into the job and she is already thinking about another woman's man? Well, who wouldn't? He's drop-dead gorgeous!

Cassie Lynn tries to convince herself that maybe his flirtatious way was to try and make Juliana jealous, or maybe he's just a playboy and sought another skirt to chase. Oh well, who knows. He's definitely out of her league—as she recalls her dorky somewhat boyfriend in Austin whom she recently dumped. Continuing with her typing she reminds herself to focus on her career and forget about the opposite sex until the right guy comes along.

Chapter Six

The Fear of Living Alone

Before leaving work that day Cassie Lynn takes time to slap her parking sticker into the upper corner of the windshield, now showing that she is legal to park inside the plant. The drive home is pleasant with no road rage occurring and upon arriving home remarkably no one is parked in her assigned parking spot. Moving in, she experienced folks breaking the rules always parking wherever they liked and as proven, her spot is one of the most convenient for rule breakers. Its 5:46 pm and her stomach is growling, and she is hungry after a busy and somewhat exciting first day.

Quickly, she scurries up the stairs to her apartment and once inside locks the door behind her. She sits her attaché case down near the door and makes her way toward the bedroom, time to get comfortable and then chow down on something more delicious than what she had for lunch. Entering the hallway and before reaching the bedroom she catches a whiff of something faint lingering in the air and her instinct tells her to stop. The odor is extremely faint, and when unable to determine what it is and with nothing coming to mind, she continues forward to the bathroom. After that, she sits on the side of the bed, kicks off her shoes and rubs her feet, which are sore after wearing them all day. Indeed, wearing new shoes can be painful and a little foot massage with lotion can bring some relief. With the circulation and soreness addressed, she wipes the excess lotion onto her arms. She notices a pair of her black panties lying at the foot of the bed. She picks them up and also notices the top drawer of the dresser slightly ajar. This is not good. Cassie Lynn is a perfectionist borderline "OCD" and would have never left the panties on the bed with the dresser drawer ajar.

Puzzled by what she sees, her thoughts return to the faint odor in the hallway, and instantly fear engulfs her. She begins to think that someone has been or still is in her apartment. But where?

There is no time to waste so she grabs the only weapon at hand, one of those cute little pumps from the floor. Although the shoe is small and may not kill whomever, it is capable of doing a lot of damage if used correctly.

The first place she looks is under the bed, then with shoe held high and ready to strike she scans the closet, and no one is in there either. Shaking in her britches she moves into the hallway; the attic door is locked secure and no one hides in the hall closet where the washer and dryer are located. From the hallway she moves into the bathroom and cautiously peeks behind the shower curtain. Still no one. Last, she finds the kitchen has not been disturbed. What a relief, she is safe.

After playing detective Sherlock Holmes she places her black panties back into the dresser then slips on her "Tweety-bird" night shirt and tries to calm down while munching on a TV dinner and ice-cream sundae drenched with chocolate fudge on top. Oh Yeah, an ice-cream sundae for dessert and drenched in chocolate fudge, and well deserved wouldn't you say. Now, the fun part comes, while watching her favorite game show, there is no need to get up and get a napkin or wash the smeared chocolate from her lips, her tongue is the perfect napkin and will work just fine.

When all is cleaned up in the kitchen she can't seem to shake the thought of her panties being on the bed, and wondering if she had left them there by mistake or did someone from management enter while she was at work. Well, no need to contact the office management now they've left for the day, she'll have to check it out tomorrow. She begins to look around the apartment for a possible notification sheet stating someone had entered during the day but after tables, chairs, and floor areas are searched, she finds nothing. The phone rings, and awe, a pleasant surprise, its Uncle Randy and he wants to hear how the first day at work went. She doesn't share all of the details at first and keeps the conversation pretty much on business matters, but by the tone in her voice Uncle Randy picks up on a few things that concern him.

Uncle Randy Asks?

Niecie, (as he calls her) what's bothering you. I don't like the tone in your voice, fill me in.

Cassie Lynn breaks down and tearfully shares everything,

even the incident in the wee hours of the morning, and he's not happy with what he hears. Uncle Randy is slow to react, listening carefully, and when he finally does react he insists that she calm down, and states it's possible someone came in to change the air-conditioner filter or check the fire alarm and forgot to leave a notice of entry. After he learns that a notice of entry was not found he wants her to call management first thing in the morning and depending on what they say he has an idea on what needs to be done next. Cassie Lynn finds some comfort in what he says, and they plan to talk again, tomorrow evening. Her shoe now sits on the nightstand for protection and throughout the night she tosses and turns not resting much and concerned about what may happen next.

Morning comes and thankfully nothing did happen, no one woke her up crying but, she feels sluggish and not a good way to start the second day on the job. At work she gulps down more than her fair share of coffee trying to keep her eyes open while working on some late purchase orders from yesterday. When 10:00 rolls around she immediately gives the apartment manager Dottie Stevens a call, and unfortunately no one entered her apartment yesterday. Concerned by what Cassie Lynn has shared, Dottie strongly believes that she left the panties on the bed by mistake, but she does ask Cassie Lynn to call her immediately if anything else occurs to that nature.

So, with that bit of information and not exactly what she wanted to hear Cassie can't help but wonder what Uncle Randy has up his sleeve. Well, whatever he has in mind she will have to wait until tonight as she continues with her work and for lunch, it's going to be another visit to the vending machine. On the menu for today: a ham and cheese sandwich with those tasty salt and vinegar chips which she just can't seem to get enough of. After her gourmet sandwich and chips are eaten the clock on her wall shows that she has time for at least a twenty minute power nap for dessert, and after another restless night and not much sleep, she chooses to do just that. With the door closed the door mini blinds will provide the privacy needed for napping. Thankfully, no one disturbs her, and the power nap definitely helps, and afterward she manages to get caught up with her work and then some, but it's obvious she needs more Z's to get caught up on sleep. Soon the clock on her desk reads 4:53, and like all employees throughout the building they are anxious for 5:00

to roll around. It seems everyone is full of excitement and ready to party as tomorrow starts a three-day holiday, a July 4th, celebration which she plans to lounge around for most, if not all, just relaxing. Once home she does a thorough search of the apartment and with all secure and nothing out of place, she watches the evening news. With everything that happened yesterday and while she listens to the world's drama, it's time for something more enjoyable. A hot bubble bath seems to be appropriate, and with candles lit and lining the tub a few more sit about in the bathroom, some on the toilet tank and sink area. Submerged in luxury with bubbles up to her chin a clock radio on the nightstand plays calming music which sets the mood for relaxing. After almost falling asleep and with her fingers starting to wrinkle from the warm water, she drains the tub, heaven forbid she doesn't want to drown like some of those folks in the movies.

The bubble bath was fabulous and after blowing out all of the candles, nine to be exact, it's time to give Uncle Randy a call. She fills him in on what the apartment manager said and how unlike yesterday nothing was out of place when she got home from work. All is pleasing to his ears, and like management he too is starting to think she could have left the panties on the bed by mistake, but he firmly believes that she needs something more than just a shoe to protect herself. Yikes, he wants her to buy a gun. Reluctant to admit that he is right she knows that her parents would have a fit if they ever found out. He reminds her, ok Cassie Lynn, remember, you're an independent woman, adult, so now with that said you are entitled to secrets and they need not know. So, with a three-day holiday in progress Uncle Randy convinces her to start shopping and not to worry about the cost, he's got that covered. He wired funds to a local gun shop earlier that day and the funds will not only cover the cost of a gun and permit to carry but, he insists that she be trained to use it by a professional. Seems there's no need for Cassie Lynn to figure out what to do next, because Uncle Randy has her back and he wants her safe, and to be safe immediately.

Well, no time to lounge around and get caught up on sleep, the next morning she sets out first thing to shop for a gun. On her way out the door and as she makes her way down the stairs to her car, she sees a few of her neighbors socializing and walking their dogs. She meets her first neighbor Betty Tackett who lives next door to her and in the opposite apartment of "The man that cries out in the night." She is a single Mom with a newborn baby, recently divorced, and works part time. After a little small talk, she escapes to her car and drives down South Padre Island Drive also referred to as (S.P.I.D. and SH 358) looking for the gun shop Uncle Randy recommended. Once inside her ID is checked and the owner Dave informs twenty-year-old Cassie Lynn about the Texas rules and laws when purchasing a firearm. He starts with the required background check, then explains anyone eighteen or older may purchase a long gun, and anyone twenty-one or older may purchase a handgun. A brown leather case with combination lock lies on the counter. Dave removes a Ruger LCP handgun, purple, lightweight Caliber 380 Auto, and with a price range of $350. He proceeds to open and close the cartridge, aims across the room, pulls the trigger, and then flips on the safety lock before placing it into Cassie Lynn's hands.

Dave Says,

So, what do you think about this little "Purple Jewel" young lady?

Why of course she loves it, purple happens to be one of her favorite colors but, when it comes to self-defense will it do the job and protect her under the "Stand Your Ground" Law? The owner explains no complaints yet, he chuckles while she fumbles with the gun from one hand to the other. It seems she's pleased with "The Little Purple Jewel" and how it feels in her hands. Like some folks and when one holds a gun for the first time, they sometimes experience power, confidence, and Cassie Lynn turns into one of those people. She is ready to try it out on the shooting range but not so fast. There's one thing that stands in her way, she's three months shy of the legal age, twenty-one. Disappointment covers her face and wonders will Dave hold it for three months? Oh, yes indeed he will, Uncle Randy has already paid for the gun and everything involved with having one. Yep, the entire package along with a personal message "Happy Birthday!" and it is all hers. That brings a big smile to her face. The excitement of owning her own gun is so cool, but having to wait to take it home is a bummer, and as much as she'd love to take "The Little Purple Jewel" home, she does understand, gotta follow the laws of the land, right? She can only hope that the three months will go by fast, with no more incidents at home. Also, this will give the owner Dave at the gun shop time to run the background check, get her permit to carry, and set up classes for her at a local shooting range.

Dave Says,

You know young lady, when I was growing up, I sure wished I'd had an Uncle like yours.

Driving home and anxious to get there she can't wait to call Uncle Randy and thank him for the birthday present. For two years now she has been labeled an adult by society, and now she truly feels like one. She's a soon to be gun owner. Once home, it seems lady luck is on her side again, as there are no rule breakers parked in her spot, and while exiting her car, a convertible, classy cherry-red sports car, whips into the parking spot next to hers.

Not using the car door, the guy behind the wheel jumps out, and proceeds to walk with her towards the apartments. She can't help but think, who is this guy and what does he want? Not sure if she should run for her apartment or turn and flee running the other way, she's just not sure what to do. When she spots a few more folks out and about, that seems to ease her suspicions, feeling that he wouldn't do her any harm with others around, or would he. As they continue to walk Cassie Lynn can't seem to get a word in edgewise. This guy is a real yacker, arrogant, and slightly flirtatious and if that's not enough he even knows which apartment she resides in. Well, that's a red flag, wouldn't you think!

Once at the stairway leading to her apartment, the guy finally introduces himself. He is Jeffrey Martin and he lives in the apartment below hers. After she shares her name, he proceeds to tell her, somewhat bragging, that he is a body builder and instructor at a local gym in town. While Jeffrey continues to yack, Cassie Lynn begins to look around, bored by his love of self, she catches a glance of someone peeking through the mini blinds in the apartment next to hers. It's "The man that cries out in the night's" apartment, and whomever it is, they seem to be watching her and Jeffrey.

Soon, Jeffrey gets distracted by a friend and Cassie Lynn makes her way up the stairs to her apartment and she notices whoever was watching earlier, isn't anymore. After she calls Uncle Randy thanking him for the early birthday gift she decides to take a little drive around town, she wants to learn more about her birth town Corpus Christi, and possibly locate the home where her birthmother lived before giving birth to her. For two years now and after learning about her birthmother's story she has desired to speak with the Superior Nun Frances May Elliott and find out where exactly her birthmother is buried. As she makes her way down Shoreline Drive, she decides to stop at Spohn Hospital, hoping to locate Frances May. Once there, right away she hits a stumbling block as a Medical Records employee at the hospital informs her that Frances May passed away approximately ten years ago and the home for unwed mothers no longer exists. With the news difficult to hear, where does she go from here? It seems there is no one to be found that can help her, so at this time in her life it is essential that she hold on to the story that her parents shared a couple of years ago and search for more information when time allows. Call it a sign from above she passes a chapel on her way out of the hospital and there on the wall is a plaque honoring Frances May Elliott and all that she did for unwed mothers in Corpus Christi. What a pleasant comforting thing to see since she already knows that this woman cared for her birthmother and made sure she was adopted by a loving family.

What a busy day Cassie Lynn had. She met a few neighbors, bought a gun, and toured Corpus Christi. The next day is equally exciting. She watches the fireworks show on shoreline, and on Sunday morning she attends a Church of Christ on South Staples. Thankfully, there aren't any more incidents allowing her to sleep through the night and she even gets to work in a few much needed, extra naps.

Chapter Seven

Say Hello to the Little Purple Jewel

With "The man that cries out in the night" retreating to total silence and with no more incidents occurring, being able to sleep throughout the night makes a big difference in her busy routine. Months go by, and the Fourth of July holiday is now in the past and life falls into somewhat normalcy. Cassie Lynn's routine is pretty much… work, grocery shop, attend church on Sundays, pay the bills and repeat the same routine all over again. Also, she is a frugal person like her folks, with her bank statements beginning to prove that life is great as an independent woman. Soon, the October cool fronts begin to blow in and the leaves on the Chinese Tallows begin to show signs, bright red, yellow and orange leaves confirming that winter is on the way. During the changing of the leaves, folks at work and around the apartment complex decorate for Halloween, but not Cassie Lynn. This upcoming Halloween her main focus won't be on tricks and treats, but becoming an adult at the ripe old age of twenty-one, and the first thing she is going to do, is pick up "The Little Purple Jewel" from the gun shop. Unlike others her age, turning twenty-one on Halloween would call for a big party celebration, going out on the town to party and drink and God only knows what else, but that's just not "Little Miss Independent's" style.

On Saturday October 31st, her birthday, she's at the gun shop early and waits for Dave to open up so she can pick up "The Little Purple Jewel." Once she is legal to walk out the door with receipt, permit, admonition, and "The Little Purple Jewel" in hand, she plans to drive way out Weber (also referred to as WOW) to "Shorty's Bulls-Eye Shooting Range." Thanks to Uncle Randy, that Dave took care of everything even the personal lessons with a guy named Shorty, a good friend of his. He is the owner and a firearm training instructor, better yet, a sniper marksman from the Vietnam War. So, who more could a rookie gun owner need? Yep, Dave and Shorty, the two have been buddies for years and when Shorty heard how much money was involved with teaching Cassie Lynn how to shoot and clean her gun properly, for sure he is ready and willing to step up and be a personal trainer.

Cassie Lynn drives slowly down Weber and once she reaches the outskirts of town there's a sign that leads her to the shooting range. In the parking lot she sits in the car for a few minutes and is amazed by all of the young and older folks coming and going. Seems the jitters have overwhelmed her, she's nervous and her stomach begins to knot up. I would say that's more than natural since she's never owned or used a gun before. After a few deep breaths, she grabs her gun and heads towards a rusty singlewide trailer with a neon sign above the door that says, "Shorty's Office." Up the porch steps she goes and before she can reach the door it swings open and there standing in her way is a huge, downright dirty looking man, and I mean W.W.F. huge.

Startled by his sudden presence, she gasps, and those hazel green eyes of hers pop wide-open resembling large marbles. With one look at this character and while choking on her own spit, it's clear not even her petite frame will squeeze past this guy; he totally fills the entire door frame. Well what a shocker, Cassie Lynn meet your personal instructor, Shorty. This is not what she was expecting a shooting instructor to look like, and some would say, and as true as it may be, never be deceived by someone's appearance or judge a book by its cover. Just because Shorty looks tough and rugged, he's not, he's a big old friendly teddy bear, and one might even call him "Gentle Ben".

Author:

Here's a little trivia… Remember that television series back in the late 1960's? If not, the series was about an American family (The Wedloe's) living in the Florida everglades with a huge 650-pound black grizzly bear for a pet and his name was "Gentle Ben". Ben was friendly, gentle, and most of all loveable to young Mark Wedloe played by Clint Howard.

So, with that said when it comes to Shorty and his raggedy welder's hat and dirty jeans which he wears below what seems to be a beer gut, he is no grizzly bear but he does have a gentle soul. After a little small talk Shorty walks Cassie Lynn over to a shooting booth and the first thing he does is have her unlock the case. Once the case is open, he removes "The Little Purple Jewel" and it seems the small talk is over as he begins the first lessons of seven and possibly eight.

Shorty Says,
Purple is becoming to you, young lady.

Cassie Lynn Replies,
Thank you it's one of my favorite colors.

With gun in hand Shorty begins to do what he does best, starting with the required basic rules, if it's raining don't bother to show up as we will be closed. But, when open, wear flat shoes, long pants and layers of shirts when cold, and absolutely, no camouflage. He also informs her that 40 to 60 percent of women account for all classes at his range but she happens to be the first and only woman he's given lessons to. With that said, he places "The Little Purple Jewel" in her hand, and with her being a first-time gun owner he walks her through loading and unloading the gun. When she's got that down, he has her reload the gun, hands her some ear plugs and tells her it's time to see how good her aim is. While watching her stance and with the way she looks, he's betting she misses the entire target with the first shot, and sure enough his prediction is right, she misses and shortly after disappointment covers her entire face.

Shorty Says,
Well, young lady not to worry I've seen worse. Keep shooting. That target isn't going anywhere.

With the first lesson behind her and unsure if she should be using a gun, at home she searches for a safe and secure place to store it. Soon, she decides on the bottom drawer of her nightstand, as it sits empty and will work for the time being. Her plan is to keep it locked up safely during the day and remove it for scheduled lessons and before retiring for the evening. From now on, and at bedtime she plans to remove it from its case, and then lay it on top of the nightstand within reach. With "The Little Purple Jewel" now in a safe place someone knocks at the door, and it is a few trick or treaters from around the apartment complex. After opening the door to a few, she decides to call it a night when the last little goblin gets more candy than anticipated. Shortly after, she locks up, flips the lights off and retreats to the bedroom. Still feeling a little uncomfortable with a gun in the house she decides to wait until Monday before implementing her bedtime plan. So, she jumps into bed, and cuddles up with a good book before falling asleep. After a few weeks of lessons out of the way, she is becoming more than comfortable with her "Little Purple Jewel," and as proven Shorty was the right person to see when it came to being trained properly. She's able to hit still and moving targets in a blink of an eye, never hesitating.

With the up-and-coming holidays on the calendar she plans a few trips to Austin, wanting to spend time with family and friends. When doing so, she chooses to hit the airways besides the roadways, which makes the trips less stressful. Upon returning after Christmas, and with more than her fair share of gifts she unloads her car, and places them in the little walk-in attic to sort through them on another day. Way too tired to do it now, she knows it will take too long to figure out which gifts are going to be keepers and others re-gifters. While in the attic and as she stacks them neatly, she gets an eerie feeling as if someone is watching her. Quickly she finishes, and then shuts and locks the door behind her, and never gives it another thought. With "The Little Purple Jewel" sitting on top of the nightstand, sleep comes quickly after she hits the bed and there is no need to count sheep tonight. Shortly, and after she has drifted off into a deep sleep, she stirs a bit, and with heavy eyelids she opens her eyes and there standing in the doorway of her bedroom is a dark figure. Frozen, she closes her eyes for a minute hoping she is just seeing things and after opening them again, no one is there. The dark figure is gone or was is it ever really there.

In a matter of seconds she scoots up in bed and now sitting at the headboard she reaches over and grabs "The Little Purple Jewel," flips off the safety, and into the darkness of the night she proceeds to search her apartment. As a dim light shines through the mini blinds she maneuvers her way through each room with her gun positioned and ready to fire, and still there is no one in her apartment. With her mind racing and now feeling like an idiot, she convinces herself that she must have been dreaming, and imagining what she thought she saw. With "The Little Purple Jewel" back on the nightstand she lies in bed, watching the door and when she can't keep her eyes open anymore, she drifts off sleeping until the alarm goes off. It's Monday December 28th and she sits at her desk sipping on a cup of coffee when Jayleen comes into her office and flops down in the chair in front of her desk.

Jayleen Asks?
On Thursday, are you going to the New Year's Eve party at Juliana's house?

Cassie Lynn Replies,
I had no idea I was invited.

Jayleen informs her, that every year there is a party and all department employees are invited, some show up and some don't. She continues to tell her it's the must go to party of the year, with live music, food and drink provided. With that said Jayleen hands her directions to Juliana's house and suggest that if she ever wants to advance with the company, she may want to show up and mingle with the big boys and girls.

Cassie Lynn Says,
Well, it seems I have plans for a New Year's Eve Shindig, wouldn't you say.

Jayleen Replies,
Seems you do friend, see ya there.

As Jayleen walks out of her office, she gives a shout out to Cassie Lynn, wear something fancy girl, and make sure you dress to impress. So, with her New Year's Eve celebration all planned out by "Miss Stilettos" and with nothing in her wardrobe at home that comes close to the word fancy, it seems over the next few days, her evenings will be spent at the mall searching for something elegant to wear.

Chapter Eight

A New Year's Eve to Remember

When at the mall, the party dresses are in abundance, with many stores having an entire floor full of all kinds of styles, shapes, and sizes, and after thumbing through many racks, it's quite clear finding something fancy that suits her personality is going to take some time. With many dresses revealing more than she likes it seems someone slipped a cute, somewhat fancy or maybe not so fancy, little black shifty dress in with the sexy ones and no need to look further, the cute little black shifty dress will work just fine. Sure, it's a plain looking dress, with its turtleneck, long sleeves and calf length hemline, just throw in some accessories, and it will have sexy little lady written all over it. She purchases the dress and then strolls down the mall in search of black high heels to match, when she comes across a pair of three-inch black patent high heels displayed in a showcase window. Stopping to check them out, yikes, the price tag is not what she wants to pay, and contemplating whether to splurge or not to splurge, she splurges leaving the mall with what she considers to be, a somewhat fancy and sexy outfit.

On Thursday, New Year's Eve and while at work the talk around the building is all about the big shindig tonight, the 1993 New Year's Eve party at Juliana's house. It seems folks are anxious and ready to party, with many bragging on what they will be wearing and how much they spent to look sexy and fabulous. For lunch, Cassie Lynn raids the vending machines and while stopping at a nearby watering hole, for a sip of water, Juliana and Maxine happen to walk by, and of course Juliana wants to know if she is coming to her party. As for Maxine, she doesn't say a word she just stands there and glares over those dark rimmed glasses still dangling on the tip of her nose, and more than likely she is wondering what Juliana's reaction will be when Cassie Lynn answers.

Cassie Lynn Says,

Sure, I'm looking forward to it Juliana, and I'll see you tonight.

When Cassie Lynn gets back to her department, she walks in and finds Jayleen bubbling with excitement. She informs her, the plant manager has just authorized that all administrative employees may leave at three o'clock, giving everyone time to get ready for the party. This news is perfect, she scurries to her office and with not much time left to tie up a few loose ends, she addresses a few of those most important matters and then flies out the door with others ready to celebrate the arrival of another New Year. Before she heads home to dress for the party she takes a dry run out to the "Wood River" subdivision where Juliana lives as it's better to know where you're going than not, and after finding her house it's obviously Juliana is living large. By the looks of her house and the subdivision, it seems this is going to be some kind of party.

As she heads home and with no time to get a fast Mani and Pedi on her way home she stops by a corner five and dime, picks up a tube of dark red lipstick and fingernail polish to match, desiring to bring a little color to her lips and fingernails. Also, and before checking out she grabs a bundle of assorted flowers which she plans to take to Juliana as a hostess gift. Once home she polishes her nails immediately and when dry she jumps into the shower. Afterwards she moisturizes her legs, feet, and elbows, and then gives a little spritz of musk perfume into the air, allowing the fine mist to land where needed. Sitting at bedside she now tugs and pulls on a pair of black stockings and once the wrestling match is over and they're adjusted with no kinks, over her head she slips on the not so fancy little black dress. The high heels follow and the view in the mirror is not a good one. The all black idea comes across as if she were going to a funeral and not a fancy New Year's Eve party. So, it's time to make some changes and make them fast, and no need to freak out, hanging nearby is an oversized bright pink wrap that will work just fine, as it's cool outside. Before wrapping it around her shoulders, she pulls from her jewelry box two long strands of white pearls and matching teardrop earrings to match. She maneuvers the long strands of pearls at different lengths giving them and her outfit a more 70's look, and when she is pleased with that certain look, she clips on the earrings. Finally, she is ready, and it is time to get going and have some fun.

When Cassie Lynn finally arrives and running late as usual, finding a place to park isn't easy, and unlike earlier the street is totally packed with numerus cars. Upon approaching the door a few other folks follow and as the door opens a butler stands and offers to take her wrap. But she chooses to leave it on as she's a little chilly. Standing nearby is the hostess Juliana looking like a movie star and also decked out in a little black dress but hers is short, glitzy, and revealing with a low-cut neckline. Talk about wanting to be the center of attention and leaving something (nothing?) to the imagination, well not tonight as Juliana chose to display the sexy look with her bosom bulging, popping, and basically pouring out from under her little pushup bra.

Author:

Juliana, you best be careful, because as sexy as you think you may look, with one wrong move, it's possible, you could find yourself flashing a few or all of your guests.

With folks stirring about she makes her way over to Juliana and hands her the flowers of appreciation, and most of all, for inviting her into her home. Rudely, Juliana takes them and tosses them onto a nearby table. Then, without saying a word, she gives her a hateful snobby look as she looks her over from head to toe, and then deliberately moves on to welcome others arriving through the door. Soon, Maxine appears from out of another room.

Maxine Says,

Well, it seems you should have declined the invitation, because sweet is not in Juliana's vocabulary and, you will never win her over with sweetness. Excuse me while I take care of the flowers for our rude hostess.

Soon the house is packed with partygoers and after maneuvering her way into the family room and what's called the den in the south, she finds the bar, and then mingles around while sipping on a diet coke. She spots Jayleen and her husband Malcolm all decked out in their fancy attire. Laughing and carrying on, soon Maxine appears out of nowhere and joins in on the fun. Not long into their conversation Maxine sorta, maybe kinda, apologizes for Juliana's behavior.

Cassie Lynn Says,

No need to apologize Maxine, I'm fine, I learned at a very young age not everyone is going to like you.

For several hours people drink, cut up, and mingle amongst themselves, and when a wall clock over the fireplace mantel dings 11:30, that means the New Year is thirty minutes away. With that warning the partygoers get louder and totally rambunctious, even Maxine displays a little wild streak. Like I've mentioned before she may be old but she ain't dead, when she performs a little "Boogie-Woogie" dance over towards Cassie Lynn and surprise, it's Dion Martine and he is dancing with her. Jeepers, where in the world did he come from, and does Juliana know that he is here? Immediately, Cassie Lynn begins to scan the room looking for Juliana, and where is she, no worries as she is across the room, cuddled up in a corner laughing and carrying on with other male party goers. So, with Dion being Juliana's ex, and her off in a corner carrying on with a few other liquored-up folks that means, Dion is fair game and before Cassie Lynn can say a word Maxine pushes Dion into her arms and leaves them to finish out the slow dance. Dion doesn't waste any time as he pulls her in close, and with his arms now wrapped around her waist, is she going to push him away or not?

Dion Says,

Why hello again, little Purchasing Agent Cassie Lynn Dawalt.

Whispering in her ear he tells her, I must say, you look lovely in your little black dress and pink wrap. You may not remember, but I recall telling you the first time we met, "Maybe I'll see you again sometime," well, here I am, here to see you and only you. No need to tremble anymore, you can relax as I'm not one to bite and as you've seen Juliana is pretty much occupied, wouldn't you say.

With one slow dance after another, and with the big countdown about to start, Dion continues to hold on to the woman that he desires to kiss at twelve o'clock. Soon, folks begin to whoop and holler as the countdown begins, ten, nine, eight, seven, six, five, four, three… well, hold on to your heart Dion, when one follows two, neither Dion nor Cassie Lynn hears the screams of "Happy New Year."

Their lips lock together in a kiss to remember.

With horns blowing, and balloons bursting with confetti floating all about the room the two love birds finally come up for air, and nearby Cassie Lynn finds Maxine and Jayleen, smiling, and guilty as sin, and it seems these two are responsible for the unexpected kiss. By the looks on their faces it seems they've been planning this little hook up for some time. Oh boy, look out Cassie Lynn, it seems you have stolen someone's "New Year's Eve kiss" and the so-called victim is not happy. As you might have guessed, here comes Juliana pushing her way through the crowd, with her half-full champagne glass slushing about, and she is determined to nab Dion away from Cassie Lynn's company. Within seconds, she nudges her way in between them both, explaining to Dion that it is vital that he meet a few realtors moving into the area and before they leave the party. Dion, a well-known broker in town is not the least bit happy with the timing but doesn't want to pass up an opportunity to engage with a few new realtors, either.

Author:

Well, what a clever move on Juliana's part, and I wonder what her next move will be when it comes to keeping Dion and Cassie Lynn apart.

Once Juliana has Dion back under her thumb, many folks start to leave with Cassie Lynn planning to do the same. Disappointed that she didn't have more time to learn about Dion or say goodbye, she does say good-bye to Maxine and Jayleen, asking that they give Dion a message on her behalf, and of course they are all ears, anxious, and ready to hear what she has to say.

Cassie Lynn Says,

I'll make this short and sweet; just tell him, "Maybe I'll see you again sometime"?

Author:

Well, I don't know how you may feel about that message, but

as for me, sounds like a plan.

Relying on her buddies to pass on the message, she slips out the front door and leaves the party without seeing or saying a word to Juliana or Dion. Now 1:00 in the morning, she cautiously makes her way down I-37, and as she drives, she keeps a sharp eye out for possible drunk drivers. When she arrives home, she finds a few residents from the apartments still up, celebrating, as they drink and shoot off illegal fireworks. Once she is safe and inside her apartment, she goes straight to bed, and then lays there in the dark reminiscing about that romantic New Year's kiss from Dion's lips, and oh what a kiss it was. Yes indeed, that kiss was like none other than she has ever experienced, and for sure, ten times better than her somewhat dorky ex-boyfriend from Austin could have ever put out. Over the weekend most of her time was spent daydreaming and wondering if Dion's interest in her, is sincere. Her gut tells her yes, but then there's that ex, the cougar Juliana who continues to stand in the way.

Author:
Be careful Cassie Lynn, it's proven that two-legged cougars can be just as dangerous as four.

When Monday comes, Cassie Lynn speeds to work, anxious and hoping to hear what Dion had to say about her message, and upon arriving, there is no need to look for her buddies Maxine and Jayleen because one of them, already sits, waiting in her office for her. It's Maxine, and she doesn't waste any time, she just gets to the matter at hand, and begins to share what happened after she left.

Maxine Says,
Girl, you must know, yours and Dion's kiss was the talk of the party and when you left, Juliana wasn't happy when she saw you and him locking lips.

Cassie Lynn Says,
Please Maxine, enough about Juliana, did you give Dion my message.

Oh yes, Maxine tells her, I passed the message on to Dion

and his reaction was a smile, and with Juliana near keeping him occupied, he couldn't say much. Wishing she had more to say on Dion's behalf, she makes a point to warn her about Juliana, indicating that she is a possessive individual and if she can't have Dion for herself she'll do whatever necessary to prevent another from having him. Needing to get back to HR and before she leaves Maxine suggests, warns, that Cassie Lynn keep a distance from Juliana because when it comes to Dion, her and Juliana will never be friends and don't even bother to try.

Author:
Like anyone cares!

Days pass and with nothing more than a reported smile out of Dion, Cassie Lynn can't help but think that there may be more to Dion and Juliana's relationship, and possibly, much more than she thought. So, with no word or message from him she is starting to feel like an absolute fool, and if that isn't bad enough, her buddies, Maxine and Jayleen, totally distance themselves from her and anything related to Dion and Juliana. Puzzled by the about-face from her buddies, and the dirty looks from Juliana, Cassie Lynn focuses on her work and retreats from a possible relationship with Dion.

When a few weeks go by, and with Valentines and cupid arrows filling the air, she tries desperately to focus on her work, but focusing becomes more and more difficult with thoughts of the Dion kiss getting in her way. Oh my goodness, that kiss, that kiss and oh what a kiss it was, that kiss was like none other than she has ever experienced, and it seems that the ex of Juliana's, has made her totally star struck crazy. Star struck indeed, so star struck that one day at lunch she jotted down a poem on a notepad which reads…

"A Kiss for My True Love"

That kiss, that kiss, oh my goodness that kiss,
An unexpected kiss when our lips met,
A kiss to remember, was that unexpected kiss,
With thoughts of you, my heart not forget,
You kissed me once, come kiss me twice,

In silence I wait, and only time will tell,
That kiss, that kiss, and here I sit,
Longing for you and one more kiss.

Ok Cassie Lynn, it's time to get back to work, so pull yourself together, and most of all, get back to acting your age. But not so fast, it is still lunch time when an unexpected visitor walks through the door, and oh my goodness, it's Maxine and she is holding a huge bouquet of pink and red long stem roses, twenty-four to be exact. Grinning from ear to ear, she sits them on the corner of her desk and then flops down into a nearby chair and once seated, she slides Cassie Lynn a little sealed envelope. Cassie Lynn is awed by all of the beautiful roses that have just landed on her desk.

Cassie Lynn Asks
What's all of this about?

Maxine: Looking over those dark rimmed glasses, says,
Girl, just read the note.

Cassie Lynn opens the note and it is from Dion.
The note reads…

"Maybe I'll see you again sometime"? How about Friday, February 12th as I would love to celebrate an early Valentine's Day dinner with you at the Omni Hotel, and that's if you're free.
Signed…
All yours, Dion Martine.

After she has read the note, Cassie Lynn slides it back towards Maxine and makes it clear that she's flattered, but not interested. Whoops, it appears, Cassie Lynn is playing hard to get and not happy with Dion and everyone else involved with him, so Maxine needs to think fast as there are two dozen expensive roses sitting on the corner of Cassie Lynn's desk. Soon, and when those dark rimmed glasses get flipped up into her hair.

Maxine Says,
From what I've seen and heard, I can somewhat agree with your reaction, but before I leave, may I share a bit of information

with you.

Cassie Lynn Replies
Speak, I'm all ears!

As Cassie Lynn listens, she is stunned by what she hears. It seems when Juliana and Dion broke up many months ago the devil moved in and snatched up Juliana's soul. Immediately she became difficult to be around, and after being labeled a cougar during their relationship, the break up left her jealous and possessive, since they went from being a couple, to best friends with benefits, as some folks in the building would say.

Maxine Says,
Well, girl, let me make this clear, the rumors about the friends with benefits? It's just a rumor and as much as Juliana would like folks to believe it is, it's not, and I got my information firsthand from the horse's mouth: Dion.

So, with that said, she adds more to the story and makes a point to share with Cassie Lynn what happened after she left Juliana's house. With only a few partygoers lingering around, Dion and Juliana got into a big argument, and yes it was about you, and he was furious about how she treated you. He tells her that he has had enough of her games and not only are they over, but their friendship is too. With Juliana in tears, he then turns and walks out the door and never looks back. Maxine also explains that afterwards Juliana swore her to silence when it came to what happened, and with her being her boss, she did so needing to keep her job.

Maxine Says,
I can only hope that you will forgive me for distancing myself from you, but under the circumstances I had no choice.

Cassie Lynn Says,
So, from what you say it seems Dion is a free man.

Maxine Says,
Indeed, and I can honestly say, that he is. So, with everything out in the open shall I give him an answer to Friday's

date?

Jumping in with both feet and not taking time to think about what she should say or do, Cassie Lynn jots her address down on a post-it and insist that Maxine give him a little one liner along with it…

Cassie Lynn Says,
"Maybe I'll see you again sometime"?

Maxine: Smiles and says,
Girl, it would be my pleasure!

Chapter Nine

A Whirlwind of Drama Occurs

Now with the truth behind Dion and Juliana's relationship exposed, Cassie Lynn decides to stay clear of Juliana, determined to spare herself from any type of cat fight confrontation. Maxine scurries back to her desk and she can't wait to give Dion a call with the good news, but with Juliana working in her office, Maxine has to use extreme caution since Juliana has a habit of listening in on other people's conversations. With her fingers resting on the phone, she patiently waits for the right opportunity. Soon, she hears Juliana talking on the phone, perfect timing as she gets Dion on another line. Whispering, and with one hand cupped over her mouth and the receiver, she keeps a close eye on Juliana's door, and gives Dion the good news, and as expected, he is ecstatic.

After giving him Cassie Lynn's address and personal message, she needs to get off the phone and fast, because if there is one thing she doesn't need, it's Juliana creeping up on her blindside and listening in on her conversation. Surely, she wouldn't do that right? Wrong, she would since she has been known to do such in the past and proving her somewhat "Sneaky as a Snake" side. So, with Dion called and informed, as a favor to him and at his request, she later calls the Omni to make the early Valentine's Day reservations for Friday night.

Within seconds of hanging up the phone Juliana walks past Maxine's desk and she is headed to a meeting and totally unaware that her ex will be having a romantic evening with Cassie Lynn on Friday night. Indeed, it seems with no interference cupid, "Maxine", stepped up and helped Dion to pull off one of the most romantic dates of the year. With Juliana now out of the office Maxine gives Cassie Lynn a quick call and informs her that the date is confirmed, and Dion will arrive at her apartment door on Friday evening at 7:00 sharp. With Maxine knowing that Cassie Lynn is one of those show up late kinda people, she gives her a heads up… Girl, be ready on time Dion believes in punctuality.

Author:
Yikes, that's going to be a tough one. Will Cassie Lynn take her advice?

On Thursday evening and with only twenty-four hours left till the big date, Cassie Lynn reminds herself about Maxine's stern warning, and how Dion is one of those punctual kind of guys. So, with that in mind and in order to save time on Friday, she begins to pull a few items together and it seems she has found an appropriate dress for Valentines and their first date. A hook on the outside of her closet door now holds one of her favorite dresses to wear, and it's her one and only dark red dress with a white laced collar, which she often wears to church on Sundays. Unable to shop for matching shoes, she goes with the black high heels which she wore on "New Year's Eve." Not wanting to wear a coat she also lays out her bright pink wrap and pearl-drop earrings as well and hoping Dion won't notice that she has worn them before. With outfit and accessories all laid out, it's now time for bed, but before she jumps under the covers, she runs to the dining room to retrieve her Valentine roses off the table. Like lavender, she hopes the sweet fragrance from the roses will send her into a deep sleep and well rested for tomorrow's big date. Once bedded down for the night, the roses now sit on the nightstand and within inches of the "Little Purple Jewel." With the lights off, and with the sweet fragrance of rose peddles filling the room, she can't help but think of Dion wondering, is he really into me, like I am into him?

Author:
Well, give it time Cassie Lynn, give it time.

Soon, the soothing smell of rose petals sends her into a deep sleep, and not stirring once, during the night she sleeps like a newborn baby. When morning comes, that good night's sleep left her feeling perky and well rested, and she's not only in a good mood, she is in a great one. Singing and jigging about the room and as she dresses for work she can't keep her eyes off the roses, coming to the conclusion that she too should give Dion some kind of gift for

Valentine's Day, and what better gift to show her true feelings, than the poem that she wrote. During lunch and while out she buys a special card just for him and writes the poem inside signing her name, date, and year. With folks at work celebrating and discussing their plans for after work, she dares not share what hers are, not wanting Juliana to cause a ruckus. When 5:00 comes she is out the door and it's time to get home and dress for her special evening with Dion.

Then, at 7:00 sharp, there's that punctual knock at the door, its Dion and as usual he is lookin' as handsome as ever, and oh my goodness, what is he wearing? Seems Mister suave and good-looking also likes pink, wearing a pale pink shirt, black slacks, and a black leather jacket. Ooh-la-la… "Happy Valentine's Day" Cassie Lynn, real men do wear pink.

Author:

Some may argue saying, Come on, "Real guys, don't wear pink." Correction! Dion wears it well and adds a stunning masculine luscious model touch to the color.

Stepping inside his eyes and all of his attention are totally on Cassie Lynn, and it seems love is in the air because he's not interested in where she lives or how she decorates. He is the perfect gentlemen as he helps her with her bright pink wrap, and then on the way out the door, she grabs a little hand clutch with Dion's surprise inside. From Cassie Lynn's apartment the ride to the Omni downtown turns out to be more than impressive. Riding in luxury and in a Jaguar, Dion decides to take a more scenic route to dinner, driving slowly down Ocean Drive. Along the way he gives Cassie Lynn one of his business cards, and after she places it into her clutch, he holds her hand and shares his upbringing and knowledge of Corpus Christi. He is a fascinating guy, smooth talker, and after hearing some of his life adventures, she is in awe. Within minutes of arriving at the Omni, Cassie Lynn decides that this guy doesn't even come close to what she first thought several months ago, (a playboy and skirt chasing flirt). It appears that he is a romantic gentleman with a good head on his shoulders, which totally impresses her.

Author:

What a guy, looks like a male model and smart too.

Indeed, and although born in Italy and raised in Corpus Christi from the young age of three, it seems "Mister Tall Dark and Handsome" slash "Ambitious Broker," has done quite well for himself with his obvious appearance and wheels. The Omni's valet personally seems to know Dion, calling him by his first name when he exits the car.

With Cassie Lynn on his arm they make their way up to the twentieth floor where they plan to enjoy a lovely evening of white tablecloth dining and dancing. Once seated they will enjoy a fabulous meal with some of the finest white wine in town, "Domaine Faiveley," and with a price tag of $220 a bottle. When Cassie Lynn catches a glimpse of how much it costs on the wine list, she struggles, unable to tell Dion that she does not drink. So, as the server pours, filling the wine goblet half full, and not wanting to look like an odd ball, she remains silent while Dion precedes to make a toast to them and their first date.

After a few sips, well, maybe several sips, and with her taste buds craving more, it is quite clear that she needs to stop when she becomes a little silly and lightheaded. Soon, the appetizers arrive, which allows her to gently slide her wine glass out of reach so she can focus more on her goblet of water nearby. With several gulps of water down, it's not long before her normal state of mind returns, which is a good thing because here comes the entrée.

A large white plate now sits before her and the impressive presentation of steak (Filet Mignon and Lobster), is way more than she expected. After nibbling on the impressive entrée and shortly after, the dessert arrives, and she decides that this is the perfect time to give Dion the Valentine's Day card. And like most men and not expecting anything the card is a pleasant surprise. While he reads, the piano player plays a well-known romantic soundtrack to "Somewhere in Time," and sets the mood for all celebrating "Valentine's Day."

After reading the card he closes it and then slides it into the pocket of his jacket. He doesn't say a word. He just takes her by the hand and waltzes her onto the dance floor. Oh boy, oh boy, first the drinking and now the dancing, this five-star restaurant seems to be taking her down a road that she's never been down, and never has a man ever held her the way Dion is. Her two left feet stumble, and it seems there's still too much of the $220 wine lingering within her system. Dion a fabulous dancer, pulls her in close and not just close, but snuggly close, and the warmth of his arms around her are comforting, when she begins to lose self-control as he and the piano player take her into a place of ecstasy and romance. Cheek to cheek they dance when Dion whispers into her ear.

Dion Says,

I'm touched by your sweet card "Purchasing Agent" Cassie Lynn Dawalt. On New Year's I kissed you once, so is this a good time to kiss you twice?

A few seconds go by with no response…

Author:

Come on Cassie Lynn, times wasting, say something.

With not one word spoken, it seems she is paralyzed and unable to get yes out of her mouth. Not wanting this moment to pass her by, she pulls her lips around to meet his as the piano player continues to play. It seems love is in the air, as "Cupid" intervenes, and it is Deja vu all over again… "That kiss, that kiss, oh my goodness that kiss", and what a moment it is for the little "Purchasing Agent" Cassie Lynn Dawalt.

The drive back to Cassie Lynn's apartment is a quiet one, as they hold hands and listen to soft instrumental music playing on the car CD player. Upon entering her apartment, she invites Dion inside for a goodbye kiss, intending to keep that kiss private from any and all neighbors still up. With the door ajar and before she can thank him for a lovely evening, the door closes as he has her pinned up against the door kissing her uncontrollably. Within seconds she melts like putty in his hands, and not asking any questions it's obvious Dion is moving forward from kiss me once, kiss me twice, and proceeding to take the kiss to a more passionate kiss. Soon, Dion's jacket and Cassie Lynn's wrap hit the floor as the breathing gets hot and heavy. Woo-wee Cassie Lynn, hold on to your heart this man is definitely into you. Caught up in ecstasy, Dion tells her that he loves her over and over as his hands begin to roam where she is just not comfortable with them being, and once the zipper on her dress begins to slide down her back, it's time to put the brakes on. She's just not ready to go where he wants to go. In the heat of the moment she calls out several times for him to stop, but he doesn't seem to hear, and she realizes that she should have stopped this kiss sooner. With her dress now hanging off her shoulders she grabs his hands attempting to push him away.

Cassie Lynn Screams out!
Stop, stop, please stop Dion, I'm a virgin.

Author:
Talk about putting the brakes on, yep that'll sure do it.

Wow, after hearing what she says Dion is lost for words. He expected to hear her say that she loved him to, but instead she screams out that she is a virgin, and what a shocker. Well, it seems it's time to go when he picks up his jacket and her wrap from the floor, and after placing her wrap into her hands, he apologizes and walks out the door closing it behind him. With Dion gone Cassie Lynn is left in tears and is furious at herself for allowing things to get so out of hand. Now broken hearted, she truly believes that she has just lost the man of her dreams and will never see him again. Immediately, she goes to bed and while lying in the dark her tear stained pillowcase needs to be changed, but she is too distraught to do so, and after flipping the pillow to the dry side she finally cries herself to sleep.

So, after four maybe five hours of peaceful sleep, she awakes in the early hours of the morning tossing and turning with thoughts of Dion still running through her mind. She flip flops about in the bed desperate to fall back to sleep when a loud bang echoes throughout her apartment, and not to fret the "Little Purple Jewel" sits on the nightstand and is ready to be used if needed. Curious, by the faint smell of cheap cologne, she quickly turns towards the nightstand, and now as she faces the doorway too, oh my goodness, there in the doorway is the dark figure she once imagined seeing several months ago. So as then, she closes her eyes shut tight, hoping once opened it will be gone. Wrong, the dark figure is real and is now moving, rushing towards her. With no time to get to her gun…

Cassie Lynn Screams out!
Who are you, what do you want?

Well, it is obvious the dark figure isn't there to answer questions or make small talk, and within seconds he has tossed some of the covers to the floor and is in bed with her. With the box springs squeaking, and as they bounce about in the bed, she struggles to get him off, and there is no doubt in her mind what he is there for. Yes indeed, he is a rapist and he is butt naked with his piercing sex pistol, pretty much proving, to be a "FACT". While they continue to wrestle and once he has her hands pinned down…

Cassie Lynn Tells him in a furious rage**,**
Get off of me, leave me alone, get off, and get off now you fool!

Rapist Says as he covers her mouth trying to silence her,
Oh no my little "Virgin", you see, soon you will belong to me.

Cassie Lynn can't believe what she just heard, and it is obvious that this fool got into her apartment after her and Dion left for their date and was still there upon their return. With that said, her rage escalates to another level and there is no time to think about what to do next.

A little voice inside her ear tells her to react, don't wait, get to the "Little Purple Jewel" and do it now. With the little voice screaming out and saying, move, move, move, she does, reacting in an angry rage of survival. Within a blink of an eye the adrenaline which now flows throughout her body, allows her to push him off, and before she even realizes what she has done the rapist flies through the air and lands on the floor with all of the remaining covers.

Perfect timing, as this gives her the time needed to get to the "Little Purple Jewel." With him now on the floor and left wrestling about with the covers, it is quite clear that he wasn't expecting such strength from such a little woman. So, while he rants, raves and cusses like a sailor she grabs the "Little Purple Jewel." With "Little

Purple" in hand she slides herself up in bed bracing herself against the headboard, all ready and willing to fill the fool with six rounds of lead if needed.

In this short amount of time he manages to free himself from the tangled covers and is now standing at the foot of her bed, so what's it going to be, does he jump back onto the bed again and accomplish what he set out to do, or does he run? With a smidgen of daylight now peeking through the mini blinds the dark figure has a different look about him. This tall slender naked old man with gray scraggily shoulder length hair seems to be unsure as to what to do as he now looks down the barrel of "Little Purple."

Cassie Lynn orders him to kneel down in the corner of the room so she can call 911. Refusing to take orders from a woman he hightails it for the front door. Oh no, the front door, did she forget to lock the door when Dion left? She calls out for him to halt but he keeps running.

So, off the bed she goes running after him, not wanting him to escape. While making his way through the living room he stumbles and falls over a chair, and with Cassie Lynn tagging not far behind she soon finds herself tumbling over his naked butt and losing the "Little Purple Jewel" at the same time.

With Cassie Lynn now on her knees feeling about the floor and in search of her gun, the rapist heads for the front door, and as he struggles, fumbles to get the door unlocked it is obvious she did lock up after Dion.

Cassie Lynn hears the click of the padlock unlocking the door, but not so fast, because at the same time she has found "Little Purple." The rapist hears the clicking noise of "Little Purple" cocked and ready to fire. Well, unlike Cassie Lynn's orders for him to kneel earlier, he decides to take his chances on her missing as he opens and hightails it out the door.

So, out the door he goes with Cassie Lynn nipping at his heels, and he is desperate to get away from this woman who'd love to plug him full of lead. Fleeing down the stairs, Cassie Lynn now stands at the top of the stairway and she calls out to him…

Cassie Lynn Screams out,
Stop or I'll shoot!

And once again he doesn't listen, so she fires off one piece of lead, and misses. Wow, what an idiot, not even the sound of a bullet flying past his head causes him to stop as he keeps running, and within seconds a second piece of lead exits the barrel and like a rocket, it swarms through the air striking him with a fatal shot to the back and lodging inside his heart. Cassie Lynn doesn't move, she just watches as his naked limp torso tumbles to the bottom of the stairway.

Author:
Game over, is all I gotta say.

With the sun rising and after shots fired, a few neighbors begin to gather wanting to see what all the commotion is about. First to emerge from behind closed doors is Jeffrey Martin, Cassie Lynn's neighbor from downstairs. Once outside he finds a man lying at the bottom of the stairs, naked as a Jaybird, and Cassie Lynn standing at the top, with a gun still dangling from her fingertips. Tending to the man's needs first and not finding a pulse, he realizes that Cassie Lynn has just shot one of their neighbors. Once Jeffrey has determined that the guy is dead, he makes his way up the stairs to where Cassie Lynn still stands. She is in shock and crying uncontrollably.

Cassie Lynn Can only say**,**
He tried to rape me. I'm sorry, but he tried to rape me.

With the police and paramedics arriving on the scene, Jeffrey removes the gun from her hands and lays it next to a handrail nearby. Soon, Betty Tackett the neighbor next to Cassie Lynn shows up with a blanket to keep her warm. As they both try to comfort her the police make their way up the stairs with guns drawn and immediately, they retrieve the weapon and take the shooter into custody. With Cassie Lynn being escorted down the stairs other officers begin to tape off the crime scene, when the paramedics inform an officer in charge that a coroner will be needed. With Cassie Lynn now in handcuffs and before being placed into a police car, she asks that her clutch be retrieved from her apartment. She tells them that the wallet inside along with a few other IDs will help to identify her. She also wants someone to call her parents. When a female investigator Miss Lea, enters her apartment she finds near the doorway entry a small clutch and assumes this is the one Cassie Lynn was talking about, and once she has determined nothing is inside will do harm she hands it to a Sergeant Floyd overseeing the case.

When at the downtown Police Station, located at 321 John Sartain St. and North Chaparral St., Sergeant Floyd secures Cassie Lynn into a nonviolent interrogation room where she is given something to drink and spends several hours answering questions during her official statement. With several folks coming in and out of the room and wanting to know what occurred and if she knew her attacker, it all becomes overwhelming. Now, totally exhausted she is anxious to see her parents, and the door opens and there they stand. Running into their arms she cries out that she had killed a man and wants to go home, and not to her apartment but back to Austin, which they all know isn't going to happen at any time soon. With her parents now at her side, Sergeant Floyd begins to explain what was found and uncovered at the scene and basically what will happen next. He informs Cassie Lynn that her neighbor next door had obviously been stalking her for some time, finding pictures of her which seemed to be taken through a window, two pairs of underwear, and a few other items, one being a dirty old "Yanks" cap, which were all neatly placed in his room. He comments that it pretty much looked like a stalker's shrine with candles and other paraphernalia. Soon, she hears the most concerning part, he didn't enter through the front door as she already knows, but he entered through the small attic door in the hallway.

Cassie Lynn Asks,
How is that possible?

He explains to her and her parents, that the guy knew that his attic backed up to hers, and after being so infatuated by her beauty, he cut out a large drywall piece, removing and replacing it when he would come and go throughout the day and night. Sure, you more than likely kept the attic door locked, but a locked door to a criminal will never keep a criminal from using certain tools of his trade, he picked the lock. Well, this bit of information would explain all of the incidents that continued to happen after moving in, and now with so much being tossed at her, soon another unexpected visitor enters the room, and it is Dion. It seems Sergeant Floyd found Dion's business card in her clutch along with her parents and called him too. Happy to see him she jumps to her feet, runs, and then falls into his arms.

Cassie Lynn's Parents Ask,
Who in the world is this guy?

Author:
Mom and Dad meet the new man in Cassie Lynn's life. First, they learn she owns a gun, and now a strange man enters the picture. What's next!

Now that Cassie Lynn has several folks by her side, it seems she and Dion need a little privacy time, when Sergeant Floyd allows them both to step out into the hallway to talk. With the door ajar and with Cassie Lynn and Dion still in eye view, Sergeant Floyd assures her parents that she is in safe hands as Dion is madly in love with their daughter. As he lets out a little snicker under his breath, he also informs them, that he strongly believes that this guy could be their future son-in-law. With Cassie Lynn more than occupied he continues to share information with her parents, and soon they learn something extremely disturbing about her attacker.

When the disturbing news is revealed their jaws drop open and they are in awe, and who would of thunk. Not only was their sweet daughter attacked and almost raped in the wee hours of the morning by a psycho on the prowl, she ends up killing the fool to whom she has biological ties too, REALLY!

This guy just wasn't her neighbor, but he was her biological father "Fredie J. Rae," and never in their wildest dreams did they ever expect to hear that name again. When Sergeant Floyd sees their reaction to the attacker's name, he is more than curious, he wants to know more, and did they happen to know this guy personally. With Mom totally in tears Dad quietly, and not wanting Cassie Lynn to hear, he reveals the unknown secrets once shared by a Nun named, Frances Mae Elliott.

Now, it's time for Sergeant Floyd's jaw to drop as well, and never in all of his years on the force has he ever heard such a disturbing story. After pulling herself together Mom asks, no she begs Sergeant Floyd, not to reveal that disturbing bit of information to Cassie Lynn, as she doesn't want her to live the rest of her life with such horrible memories of her biological father. She tells him, that it is best that he remain unknown, and as on the birth certificate, and like the Nun, Frances Mae Elliott once said, "There comes a time when secrets or promises are meant to be kept, and this happens to be one of those times," wouldn't you agree Sergeant Floyd?

Now tight lipped, and hesitant to answer, he calls Cassie Lynn and Dion back into the room while Mom and Dad sit hand in hand, sharing glances of fear, and wondering what he will say or do next. Again, with everyone back in the same room, Sergeant Floyd informs Cassie Lynn that there will be no charges brought against her and that he is releasing her into the custody of her parents.

Sergeant Floyd Says,
You are now free to go Miss Dawalt, and you may pick up your gun on your way out of the building.

Soon comes a big sigh of relief, with all ecstatic and praising the Lord, and they are excited that this entire nightmare is over. As Cassie Lynn, Dion, and her parents leave the room, Cassie Lynn makes an about face and returns to tell Sergeant Floyd that he can dispose of the gun as she will not be using it, ever again.

Sergeant Floyd smiles and **Says,**
That will be my pleasure young lady.

Upon leaving the police station, Cassie Lynn and her parents check into the Inn on Shoreline Drive, and there they plan to stay until Dion and Cassie Lynn's Dad can clear out all of her personal items. As expected, Cassie Lynn is terrified to go back into the apartment, so she and her Mom will hang out at the Inn, allowing Cassie Lynn a little time to recover, and before heading back to Austin.

Now, with this horrible ordeal behind her, and with her and Dion committed to one another, the day of leaving Corpus Christi finally comes.

Thanks to her attacker, she is no longer working at the refinery, or has an apartment lease to honor, groceries to buy and bills to pay. She can't believe how fast her life has changed in a matter of a few days, and how one fool had the capability of taking her independence away. Soon, Dion arrives and by the sparkle in his eyes love as conquered all, as he too is leaving Corpus Christi and headed to Austin with Cassie Lynn and her parents. With Dion and Cassie Lynn in his car, they lead the way driving over the Harbor Bridge, while Mom and Dad follow in Cassie Lynn's fully packed, 1988 Camry. While Dad drives, and once atop the bridge, Mom turns and looks through the back window, and begins to quote a verse from the Bible, Romans 12:19… "Vengeance is Mine, I will repay, saith the Lord".

Dad Asks,
Why that verse?

Mom Says,
At the moment I'm thinking of Cassie Lynn's biological mother and after all of these years I believe it would be appropriate to say… "Revenge is Mine, all Mine, I will repay, saith Charmaine Rene Davis."

Dad Says,
Amen, my love, Amen!

Well, after a year of issues and whirlwinds of drama, life soon gets back to normal when Dion and Cassie Lynn tie the knot in June, move to Houston and open their own business, "C & D Realtors". Now married, you may be wondering, hmmm, is Cassie Lynn walking around barefoot and pregnant yet? Well, no she is still wearing her pumps and high heels as she and Dion plan to start a family soon and in the near future, putting those plans on hold for the moment.

Author:
Well, it turns out that life is good, and **Who Wudda Thunk**!

The End

“Unforeseen Predator”

Story based on true occurrences

www.ingramcontent.com/pod-product-compliance
Lightning Source LLC
Chambersburg PA
CBHW070623310726
48982CB00001B/163

9781733469616